Advance praise for
The Alto Wore Tweed

"...The best book since the Bible..." (actual quote: "You want me to say WHAT?")
His Grace, Lord Horatio "Wiggles" Biggerstaff, ex-Bishop

"Stop calling me."
John Rutter, orthodontist, Great Falls, Montana

"If I was stranded on a desert island and could choose only one book to not have with me, this would be it. And that includes *Valley of the Dolls*."
Dr. Karen Dougherty, incidental character

"This is the most terrifying and beautiful novel I've ever read."
Edith Head (1903-1981), Clothing Designer
channeled through Madam Cleo, Psychic Hotline
($3.95 per minute)

"...Wonderful use of quotation marks. Although he [Schweizer] uses words the way a demented dentist might use a dull and rusty drill, his punctuation is extraordinary!"
Sandy Cavanah, English Professor

"Y'know, like, I mean, I really liked the part where, like, the guy, y'know did that stuff. Y'know? That was WAY cool!"
Brandi, high school honor student

"I MEAN it. Stop calling me!"
John Rutter, orthodontist, Great Falls, Montana

"I believe that with correct and careful treatment, Dr. Schweizer could eventually become a productive member of society."
Lynn Askew, Registered Nurse

"Touchingly reverent... my spirit soared...it was like *Mitford* meets *Jurassic Park* only without the wisteria and the dinosaurs."
Martha Hatteberg, alto

"If it is all the same to you, I'll read it tomorrow. The voices told me to clean all the guns today."
Robert E. Lee, Organist/Choirmaster

"Do NOT put my name on this book. I'm not joking."
Richard Shephard, composer

"Ecclesiastically disturbing..."
Tom Eblen, Methodist minister

"How did you get this number? I'm calling the police!"
John Rutter, orthodontist, Great Falls, Montana

"You got any more beer?"
Billy Hicks, lawn care professional

"If you think *this* is a liturgical mystery, you should come over to First Baptist."
Dr. Cleamon Downs, Professor of Church Music

The Alto Wore Tweed

The Alto Wore Tweed
A Liturgical Mystery
Copyright ©2002 by Mark Schweizer

Illustrations by Jim Hunt
www.jimhuntillustration.com

Published by
St. James Music Press
www.sjmp.com
P.O. Box 1009
Hopkinsville, KY 42241-1009

ISBN 0-9721211-2-9

Printed in the United States of America

4th Printing December, 2004

Acknowledgements

Thomas G. Easterling
Rebecca Watts
Sandy Cavanah
Richard Shephard
Milton Marshall

Elroy Willis — *Religion In The News*
used by permission

The Alto Wore Tweed

A Liturgical Mystery

by Mark Schweizer
illustrations by Jim Hunt

St. James Music Press
Hopkinsville, Kentucky

For the supper club

Prelude

Prelude

The UPS delivery man arrived at 4:37 p.m. I had taken the afternoon off so I wouldn't miss him since missing him would mean a trip into Boone, standing in an interminable line—something I particularly detested—and presenting my little yellow 'sorry-we-missed-you' tag to the indifferent clerk who would then spend half an hour looking for the package that was probably, by that time, back on the truck. It was my fault really, since I failed to have the shipper check the 'no-signature-required' box. Added to that, I really didn't mind taking the afternoon. It was too nice a day to be solving crime, what little there was in St. Germaine, and I was, after all, the boss. So when the UPS man showed up, I was there and happy to meet him at the door.

"Nice day, Hayden," he said, handing me the flat brown box for my electronic John Hancock.

"It is indeed," I said, noticing and appreciating again the warm fall day—the rapidly dropping humidity being the only hint of the cool weather forecast that would arrive after the sun dipped behind the blue haze of the mountains. The ever-present scent of the native fir trees seemed to be especially pungent when carried on the back of the first autumn chill and I took a deep breath, savoring the day like I might savor a good liverwurst sandwich and a bottle of imported beer — my snack waiting in the kitchen. I had all the windows and doors of the house open, trusting that with this cold front, bug season was now at its end.

I handed the box back, trading him for the package from Christie's Auction House via Philadelphia. "Thanks, Shawn," I said turning back into the house. "Have a good day."

"You too," he said perfunctorily, now busy pushing buttons on his box as he walked back to his truck.

I went into the kitchen and opened the package on the table to the sounds of the brown diesel delivery truck pulling out of the drive and heading down the road.

Inside was a typewriter. Not just any typewriter, but Raymond Chandler's 1939 Underwood No. 5. I had seen it come up in an on-line auction and had determined to get it. Underwoods weren't rare—but this one was special.

My reason for getting the typewriter, other than its obvious collector appeal, was to finally put to paper my own detective serial novella—an episodic mystery featuring a church choir director-turned-detective, written in the classic 1940's whodunit genre. In my opinion, there hadn't been a good Philip Marlowe-style mystery since 1958—the year of Chandler's last novel, *Playback,* which I had read at least four times. When he died in 1959, he left four chapters of *Poodle Springs,* but we purists don't consider the finished book a true measure of the Chandler craft. It was Ray Chandler who penned such immortal lines as *"She's a charming middle-aged lady with a face like a bucket of mud and if she has washed her hair since Coolidge's second term, I'll eat my spare tire, rim and all."*

And: *"The eighty-five cent dinner tasted like a discarded mail bag and was served to me by a waiter who looked as if he would slug me for a quarter, cut my throat for six bits, and bury me at sea in a barrel of concrete for a dollar and a half, plus sales tax."*

And perhaps his most famous: *"It was a blonde. A blonde to make a bishop kick a hole in a stained glass window."*

Sure, I could write my book on a computer. I had a couple of Macs at the house and a new iBook I was planning on taking to work, but really, what fun would that be? This was the real thing and I was feeling more than just a tingle of anticipation.

I set the old typewriter and the case of replacement ribbons that accompanied it on my desk. After I had purchased the Underwood, I had Christie's send it to a gentleman in Philadelphia who specialized in refurbishing old office equipment for collectors. It had been overhauled, oiled, fitted with a new ribbon and was now, I hoped, ready for action. I took a second to peruse the "certificate of authenticity," and then, holding my breath, I put a piece of 24 lb. white bond into the carriage and clicked the return until the edge of the paper appeared behind the hammers, slowly creeping around the roller, and finally emerging into the yellow light of the old green shaded banker's lamp I had set on the desk to complete my nostalgic foray into the Golden Age of Detective Literature. I stood and admired the typewriter for a long while. Still standing, my fingers reached for the well-worn keys and I typed

```
The Alto Wore Tweed

Chapter 1
```

I walked over to the kitchen and collected my beer and sandwich. Then, sitting at the desk, I picked up my well-worn first edition of "Farewell My Lovely" and turned to a familiar, dog-eared page.

"I needed a drink, I needed a lot of life insurance, I needed a vacation, I needed a home in the country. What I had was a coat, a hat and a gun."

Hoping some of the Chandler magic would rub off, I started typing.

The Story

Chapter 1

"Marilyn," I snarled over the phone, "did I pick the hymns this week?"

"Yes."

"Maybe you mixed up the numbers. I don't think I would have picked 'Just As I Am' for the processional."

"You picked it," she purred. "You picked it and now you've got to live with it."

I could just see her, smugly peering over her large secretarial glasses, her nimble, well-manicured fingers tapping a tarantella on her word processor. She hadn't been much help since the case of "The Soprano Wore Red," but I couldn't let her go. She knew too much. She held all the cards and they were coming up aces.

I figured she switched the hymn just to make me look bad. She didn't do it often. Just enough to keep me in my place. At least she could make a good cup of java.

"Light me a cigar and come up here a minute," I said.

"Light your own cigar." I could hear her snickering. "I'm busy."

"What'cha doing?" Meg asked, as she came into the room.

"Working on my mystery."

"Well, don't quit your day job," she admonished, offering the time-honored advice given to all aspiring writers as she ran her fingers down my spine and continued to read over my shoulder.

My "day job" happened to be police detective. Megan Farthing was my significant other, and the town beauty as far as I was concerned. I met her about three years ago, right after she had moved to town. I was off-duty at the time and on my way home in my 62 Chevy pickup for a night of Bach and grilled knockwurst when she went by me like a bullet. I flashed my blue lights, hit the siren and pulled her over a few blocks later.

"What kind of police car is *that?*" she asked, pointing to my old truck and turning on the requisite tears. "It's not really fair, is it?"

"Nope. Not fair at all. But it's a slow night. Although *you* seem to be in a hurry." I noticed the new license with the St. Germaine address. "You're new in town?"

She nodded.

"Slow down," I said, handing her license back to her. "It's just advice this time. No ticket."

The sniffling stopped almost immediately and I, once again, had to admire the female gender's ability to regulate the flow of tears in direct proportion to their chances of receiving a traffic summons.

"Are you Hayden?" she sniffed, wiping the remaining tear from her cheek and catching me totally by surprise. "My mother said I should meet you."

"Um...yes I am."

"I'm Megan. But, you know that, don't you? It was on my license." She offered me a coy smile.

I didn't know what else to say so I ventured an invitation. "Would you like to join me over at the cafe for a cup of coffee?"

"As long as it isn't viewed as some sort of police bribe for not getting a ticket."

I laughed. "I don't even have a ticket book. But don't tell anyone."

Two espressos and a couple of The Slab Cafe's beignets later, I was interested enough in extending the evening to invite her over to my place for my weekly Knock 'n Bach. The Knock 'n Bach is my standard operating procedure for staying off the dating schedule. A few ladies have attempted it, but they usually didn't last past the *Credo* of the *B minor Mass* and by now I had garnered a local reputation as a very boring date. As a result, I had not been actively pursued by the available women in St. Germaine.

Still, I had a feeling this gal was different.

"Hmmm. I like knockwurst and the sauerkraut is a real plus. How's your sound system?"

"Top notch. Marantz components. Surround sound. Two hundred watts per channel. Four Panasonic SB-MOa1 speakers."

She nodded thoughtfully. "I'd like to hear those speakers. What's on the music program?"

"*Cantata 140* and the *G-minor Organ Fugue* followed by some Leon Redbone."

"Helmuth Rilling conducting?"

"Yep." My interest went up three notches.

"God, I just love 140. The whole introduction with the three oboes and everything just sends chills up my spine."

"Yeah?" My eyes narrowed and I studied her expression. She could be bluffing, but I didn't care. "C'mon then."

It turns out she *was* bluffing, but she had sung in the Concert Choir in college and was paying enough attention in Music Appreciation 101 to fake it pretty well. I was pretty sure it was all she faked. The evening was a complete success. I was charmed by big blue-gray eyes framed by shoulder length black hair, and a figure, as they say in the South, "that would make you slap yo' mama." She's also a sharp investment counselor and a pretty darn good soprano. Lord knows, those are few and far between and worth their weight in good cigars. Sopranos, that is—not investment counselors. Megan doesn't have a solo voice exactly, but it's right on the money for choral singing and she reads like a fiend. I've always said I know a good soprano when I see one.

I pulled my fedora low over my eyes and a sneer played across my lips as I opened the hymnal looking for an old favorite containing sound theological doctrine. They were there, all right. A few of them, but they were hard to spot. Lurking in dark Bach chorales, hiding inside dimly lit Renaissance carols, stashed neatly away in the Old

Scottish Psalter. It was my job to ferret them out. Sometimes, I thought to myself, it pays to be a professional.

Meg and I've been keeping company since then and have become something of an item. She keeps track of my investment
portfolio—such as it is—something she can do on-line from her
home office. She lives with and cares for her mother, which is her
reason for being in St. Germaine in the first place. That, and having no real place to go after her divorce. Meg is smart, beautiful—
and apparently an amateur literary critic.

I sat back in my desk chair, perused the page hanging from
the typewriter, and rolled up the blue and white flannel from my
wrists to my elbows. Being a man of means but no particular fashion sense, I have three pairs of chinos and six shirts in my basic
fall and winter wardrobe. One Land's End long-sleeve white dress
shirt for Sunday and five flannel shirts of various and sundry hues.
When the weather changes, I switch to Land's End polo shirts. I
have five of those in five lovely colors: Deep Orange, Burgundy,
Chambray Heather, Sapphire and Black Forest. XXLT. $24.50. I
also have enough evening wear to cover my occasional forays into
polite society, but I don't really count that as usable wardrobe.

"I'm going to call it *The Alto Wore Tweed*," I said, sipping my
coffee and chomping on a non-lit cigar. Non-lit being the operative directive for a cigar as long as Meg was in the house.

"I'll try it out on the choir first, but I think it's pretty good. It
has all the makings of a fine detective story."

I had gotten in the habit, over the years, of channeling my
meager writing skills into missives that I placed in the back of the
choir members' music folders for their entertainment and enlight-
enment. Mostly entertainment. This was to be my magnum opus.

"You mean 'For the choir to try out during the sermon.'" She
shook her finger at me in mock derisiveness, and I attempted in
vain to look somewhat contrite.

"Hayden Konig, you're going to get in real trouble. Herself is

15

bound to see it and she'll know it's about her." She pronounced the umlauted "o" in Konig just for fun. The name is German all right, but we of the München Königs dropped the umlaut years ago in favor of everyone in our newly adopted country of the United States of America being able to pronounce it. Still, from Megan's lips it sounded wonderfully elegant and old world so I never bothered to correct her.

"It's about an alto—it has nothing to do with her," I replied.

She laughed out loud—a beautiful laugh that always reminded me of the tinkling of a zimblestern.

"Oh, I think it does. You're very transparent."

"Not a bit! I'm complex and devious. Layer upon layer of intricate, nontransparent deep stuff."

She walked out of the room, tossing her dark hair and one more comment back across her shoulder, "Says you!"

"You always offer such brilliant repartee. It's a pleasure to engage you in verbal sparring," I called after her.

Her head popped back around the corner, her eyes sparkling. "It's the *wrestling* you should be worried about. Not the sparring."

Touché. I threw a log on the fire, turned up the music, and settled back into my leather desk chair.

I put the hymnal away, my eyes narrowing as I considered the latest report from the diocese to cross my desk. There was big trouble and I knew I'd be called in to sort it out. It's what I do. I'm an L.D.--Liturgy Detective-- duly licensed by the Diocese of North Carolina and appointed by the bishop.

Suddenly I looked up and there she was--lounging in the doorway, if one could be said to be lounging in a standing position, her hair dark, dark as the elevator with the broken light bulb from which she had emerged, her eyes as brown as the three-piece suit and wingtips she was wearing. How long she had been standing there was anyone's guess. She slank slowly across the carpet.

"You know that 'slank' isn't a word," said Meg, reading over my shoulder again.

"I'm using it for effect. 'She slank slowly' is so much more descriptive than 'She *slunked* slowly.'"

"Ah, yes. Now I see."

"I'll light your cigar," she said as she leaned across my desk, a match already in her hand, her voice as husky as last year's Iditarod.

She sat on the edge of my desk, her coat falling open, revealing a tantalizing set of L.L. Bean braided suspenders. I'd seen those suspenders on sale last month, but couldn't figure a way to fit them into my continuing education budget.

"I need professional help. I'll pay you anything you want."

I hadn't had a job in a while. Not since the bishop had called me in because he suspected that someone was tampering with the lectionary. For a couple of months all the scripture lessons were either John 3:16 or Romans 3:23. It turned out that a Southern Baptist had wandered into the wrong building. I had it all wrapped up within the hour. I should have stretched the case out for a couple of weeks. It would have paid the rent.

I eyed her suspenders. I could see she was desperate. I didn't need the money, but I never could resist an alto in trouble. Especially an alto wearing tweed.

The alto that Meg was alluding to and the one I was definitely *not* writing about was Loraine Ryan—or Herself, as she was known in our choir circle—the new rector of the church. She was sent to us by the bishop to take the place, temporarily we were told, of our beloved retiring priest. Now I don't have anything against female ecclesiastics. Well, maybe a small bias—but I certainly had intended to give this one every chance. Unfortunately, this un-married militant feminist priestess had been at St. Barnabas for three months and was making no signs of looking for another position.

Directing the church choir and playing the organ for services is my part-time job, and one I enjoy. Like most church choirs, the choir of St. Barnabas isn't made up of great singers. They're bet-ter on some days than others, absent on more than a few and strictly volunteer. But I like them and the church and I can't be gotten rid of easily for several reasons: I've been there for fifteen years, I'm the only organist in town, I have a master's degree in music composition from UNC Chapel Hill, an undergraduate minor in theology and too many friends in rich places to worry about job security. Being the staff member in charge of the wor-ship service, I thought I had acted in the best interest of everyone concerned when, during Herself's inaugural Sunday, she decided that she'd like the congregation to sing *Kum-Baya* as the post-communion hymn.

When she first mentioned her plan during our worship meet-ing, I suggested to her that the congregation was used to a some-what more traditional and formal style of music, and I personally didn't much care for the campfire music of the 60's.

Mother Ryan, as she liked to be called, ignored my comments and was quite adamant. "Everyone will love it."

"I will hate it. And besides, I don't seem to have the music."

She was not to be put off. "I'll get the music. You teach it to the choir and we'll do it on Sunday."

"We generally rehearse our anthems weeks in advance, Loraine."

"Call me Mother Ryan."

"Hmmm," I said. *"This* Sunday the choir is doing Duruflé's

Ubi Caritas along with the *Veni Creator Variations*. I generally don't do the French literature, but the anthem is beautiful. It fits the lectionary and the variations can be done with the choir during communion. Also, if you check your list, you'll find we're scheduled to do the Mathias service music. Taking the service as a whole, I'm not sure that *Kum-Baya* will fit in well with all that."

She looked at me as if I was speaking to her in Swahili and had lobsters coming out of my ears. Then she smiled a cold smile.

"The Bishop and I like to have a "blended" service—some old, some new. Just go with me on this."

This was news to me. I knew Bishop Douglas pretty well. He was a traditionalist and he always gave plenty of notice in regards to his infrequent visits. But maybe he wanted to see how his new appointment was working out.

"The Bishop will be here on Sunday? Will he be celebrating?"

"Well, you never know," she said in what she perceived was a cutesy little-girl voice but came off rather like one of the munchkins from the Lolly-Pop Guild.

She was lying like Ted Koppel's hairpiece and I couldn't figure out just who she was trying to impress. She certainly wasn't impressing me and the other two members of the worship committee. Denise Franks, the lay reader for Sunday, and Beverly Greene from the Altar Guild, were old-school pillars of the church. They had grown up in the congregation, married here, had their children baptized and they, in turn, had married here also. They and their families were part of the fabric of St. Barnabas. Now they were sitting very still, not saying a word, the blood draining from their faces.

"I'll tell you what," I said, looking around in my most Grouchovian conspiratorial fashion. "I'll give you a chord and you start the song. Then I'll pick up my banjo and the choir and I will join in on the chorus. We'll just follow you." I was mugging about so much that with a cigar in my mouth and a comb under my nose, this performance would be worthy of *A Night At The Opera*.

I thought surely she would see I was being wholly sarcastic. Certainly the other two committee members knew it. She just smiled smugly and ticked the task off her to-do list. No. 3—Emasculate the choirmaster. Check.

"That will be great," she said, grinning at me like the possum that just ate the nightingale. "Everyone will love it."

"Yes, you keep saying that," I added as the committee's collective eyeball size went from ping-pong ball to saucer.

What I forgot to tell her was that I don't play the banjo. At least not in church.

What she forgot to tell me was that she was not a singer by any stretch of the definition.

And the Bishop missed the whole thing.

The exact word I used to describe Herself's unaccompanied Sunday morning solo to my good friend Tony over coffee on Monday was "interesting." The exact word most of the choir had used was "hilarious."

Father Tony Brown had retired after sixteen years at St. Barnabas. He had come to St. Germaine just a year before I did and had hired me as the organist and music director when I moved to town. There was a bit of finagling to do, such as convincing the seventy-five-year-old organist who had been there for fifty-two years that it was time to retire. But Father Tony handled everything with such aplomb that there weren't any ruffled feathers.

"She needs some time to define her own ministry," he said, sipping his coffee. "She's just defining it more abruptly than a priest with a little more experience might."

"Can we talk frankly?" I asked, getting a little irked. I had hoped for a little more sympathy.

"Nope," he said. "I have to be on *her* side. Perhaps she doesn't yet appreciate your skewed sense of humor."

"No, she might not," I said, an evil smile crossing my lips.

I had assumed she would stop singing after the first chorus

when she realized she was going on alone, but she charged ahead, glaring up at me in the balcony and singing all four stanzas—the last two in a quivering voice of rage. "Someone's praying Lord, Kum-baya." She had sounded vaguely like Ted Kennedy doing an impression of Willie Nelson on a bad day. Altogether, it might not have been the effect she was hoping for. The congregation, for some strange reason, didn't join in, but sat there, mute, as if suddenly struck dumb by the Holy Spirit.

"Sorry," I had said after the service, "I thought you were just kidding about *Kum-Baya*. But you did a great job."

She had just glowered at me, words trying to form on her lips but not making their way past her twitching jaw muscles.

"Everyone loved it," I had added.

Meg cornered me after choir practice on the next Wednesday.

"We have guidelines, Meg. Musical and liturgical guidelines," I said, mentally preparing my defense. "And we don't sing *Kum-Baya* during the worship service. The words don't even *mean* anything."

"That may be, but there's a larger issue at stake. You have to allow her some leeway in how she perceives and presents her ministry. And besides, you're the one who makes up the guidelines."

"You've been talking to Tony. And anyway, I don't make them *all* up. Some are actual guidelines agreed upon by the worship committee." I was in over my head and I knew it.

Meg leaned into me like a fighter going for the knockout. "What about the Jesus-Squeezus Rule?"

"OK. I admit I made that one up. But it's a good rule."

The Jesus-Squeezus Rule declares that the choir of St. Barnabas will never willingly sing any anthem that rhymes any word with "Jesus." The text of the offending anthem that precipitated the injunction included, "Here's to Jesus, the one who free us, just come and squeeze us." The J-Squeezus Rule was adopted unanimously by the choir and only broken once a year.

"And the exception?" She knew she had me, but I thought it was a low blow and totally irrelevant to the discussion at hand.

The exception to the J-Squeezus rule came about five Christmases ago when I, having had one too many eggnogs at the choir Christmas party, composed an anthem in which I rhymed "Holy Jesus" with "moldy cheeses." I admit that it was a bit of a forced rhyme. However, in my own defense, it was a shepherdic madrigal and moldy cheese was integral to the libretto. The choir laughed so hard in rehearsal that it was decided to grant the lovely anthem an exemption and we performed it to great acclaim at the 11:00 service on Christmas Eve and every Christmas Eve since.

I nodded, my shoulders slumping in mock defeat. "Yes, there's always an exception."

"So you can bend the rules a little..."

"You don't know her," I argued. "I've looked into her cold, serpent-like eyes. She has no soul."

"Let's just give her a chance," Meg said firmly.

During the second Sunday of her régime, Mother Ryan offered a "prayer for a womyn in her season," *womyn* apparently being the singular form of the new collective noun *wimmyn*, including a mention, among other things, of "the flowing menses of our ancient rhythms." There was a lot of squirming and sniggering going on in the bass section, and it was the general consensus that it was going to be a long winter.

"Let's just get rid of her," Meg said firmly.

The phone's unexpected ring jolted me out of my reminiscences. Meg had turned the volume up on the ringer again. I tended to leave it on "mute," explaining to Meg that I much preferred to pick up the vibrations of the phone ringing as I passed in close proximity to it—something that had never actually happened yet. And besides, if someone wanted me, I had a pager.

"The phone's for you," she hollered over the Lyle Lovett CD I had put on the Wave.

"It wouldn't be if you hadn't answered it."

"It's Dave," she yelled from the kitchen. "And you'd better get it. He says it's important."

I looked at my pager. I had turned it off. I clicked it on and it lit up like a mobile home on Christmas Eve. The police station. I decided I'd best answer the phone.

As I said before, St. Barnabas Episcopal Church is my part-time employment, but my profession in the real world is that of chief of detectives—lieutenant grade. It's an official title but, in actuality, I'm the *only* detective in St. Germaine. After discovering that "Would you like fries with that?" was the operative professional question from a guy with a masters degree in music composition, I went back to school in law enforcement and eventually got a second master's degree in public administration.

The other two cops on the force are Nancy Parsky and Dave Vance, a part-timer.

"Hayden. We've been trying to reach you."

"Just a second. Let me turn the music down. Better? Why didn't you just page me?"

"I did. I don't think you have your pager turned on."

"Hmmm," I answered, pretending to try to discover what was wrong with the offending electronics. "Ah, there it goes. Whoa. Quite a lot of messages from you guys."

"Yeah. Right, boss."

I sighed. I wasn't fooling anyone today.

"You'd better get on down here," Dave said. "Nancy's already on her way." Dave, generally a slow talker, seemed more animated than usual.

"Whoa. A three-alarmer. What's up?" It wasn't often we had this kind of action in St. Germaine. "Did Connie Ray's cows get loose downtown again?" I was joking, of course. Connie Ray's cows were only a two-alarmer. "Should I bring my gun?"

"It probably wouldn't hurt." Dave was somber and not at all

his usual jovial self.

"Jeez." I said, rolling my sleeves back down. "I'll swing by the church and get it. I left it in the organ bench."

"Organ bench?"

"I figure it might come in handy."

Dave could never figure out when I was kidding him and when I wasn't. I actually only had one of my guns in the organ bench. I kept one under the seat of my truck and the rest of them in a safe at my cabin.

"We might as well meet you there then," he said. "I'll ride with Nancy."

"Meet at the church?"

"At St. Barnabas. There's a body in the choir loft."

Dave and Nancy are both homegrown and both wanted to be on the force since they were in high school together. Dave went to the community college for a couple years, Nancy to Appalachian State where she majored in Criminal Justice. I admit that Nancy was an Affirmative Action hire, but she's worked out fine and is a top-drawer cop. She never married and so is "on call" all the time. Admittedly, there's not a whole lot of "on-calling" but she does get paid a little extra. We have one car and one cell for prisoners in the station house, but then, there isn't a lot of crime in St. Germaine. Nancy broke our big case last year—several home burglaries. Someone was breaking into houses and stealing wine. It turned out to be the McCollough boy and the story was that he was trying to get money to buy video games, which his mother wouldn't let him play anyway because they have no television set, much less a Nintendo. But the Nintendo Defense was the official version as told to Judge Adams, thus completing the plea agreement and garnering a suspended sentence. I stayed out of the whole thing since I knew the family. The wine wasn't that expensive—twenty to thirty dollars—and he rarely took more than a couple of bottles from any one house. Nancy found it all under his bed. As the kid's sister put it, "He jest ain't right and we all knows it."

Part-time Dave watches the office and takes the phone calls between nine and three. We pay him minimum wage, but he makes ends meet thanks to a small trust fund set up for him by his grandparents. All 911 calls go down to Boone and they call them back up to us.

My job is to keep everything running smoothly, which it does most of the time. When I'm feeling particularly bored or envenomed, I get my ticket book out from underneath the stacks of papers on my desk and start giving out speeding tickets around town. Unfortunately, word travels fast and traffic around town slows to a crawl until my nasty mood passes. I usually only get to give four or five tickets before all of the St. Germainites get the word. Afterwards, I tend to feel guilty and tear the tickets up. The odd person that does send in his money gets a gift certificate for breakfast downtown at The Slab courtesy of the St. Germaine Police Department. The good thing is that St. Germaine property taxes are so high that our budget doesn't depend on us producing revenue through ticketing speeders like some towns around these parts. The bad news is that our taxes are so high. I, however, don't live "in town" and thereby escape the unkind tariffs that are the lot of the rest of the unlucky serfs. Plus, I get to use the gift certificates for breakfast now and again. It's just one of my many perks.

"I gotta run," I said as I headed through the kitchen toward the back door, grabbing my sweatshirt off the nail behind the door. October tended to get chilly once the sun went down.

"What's up?" Meg looked concerned. The spinach pie and steak kabobs she'd been fixing for dinner were almost on the table. The food tempted me to leave the dead body to wait just a little longer. However, I could tell I wasn't going to get any supper without an explanation. An explanation which, if I knew Meg, would only lead to more questions—questions to which I presently had no answers.

I grabbed a kabob to-go.

"Well, little dahlin', it's time for yo' man to do some work for a change. Get your coat and a kabob and come on. I'll fill you in on the way."

Chapter 2

I slid the Rachmaninoff *Vespers Service* into the CD player as we pulled out of the drive. My blue '62 Chevy pickup, although showing its age, was outfitted with a new state-of-the-art Jansen sound system. I didn't need the big speakers because they were situated right behind my head, but I got them anyway. I flipped over to the *Nunc Dimittis*. I loved to hear those Russian basses sing that low B-flat.

"Hayden, when are you going to get a new truck?"

It was the first thing out of Megan's lips whenever she had to ride with me. She drove a three-year-old Lexus, courtesy of her ex.

"I like my truck. It suits me."

"You could get anything you want. An Expedition maybe. Or a Range Rover. For God's sake, you have over two million dollars in your accounts."

"Yeah, but this time last year I had about four. I can't afford a new truck losing two million a year."

She laughed at that. "You're not the only one who took a financial hit, you know. All the stocks took a dive. You know that when we invest..."

"We're in it for the long haul," we both sang together, chanting the mantra of the investment counselor.

The old truck was on its third transmission that I was actually aware of, and I suspected that this one was on the way out also. But I'd had the truck since '83 and I wasn't about to give it up. The odometer said 54,000, but I had put a notch in the hard plastic steering wheel every time the odometer had turned over. Added to that, it had obviously already turned over at least once when I bought it at a police auction with 24,000 showing—so I added one for good measure. Four notches so far. I hoped for at least a couple more.

"Where are we going in such a hurry that we left the spinach pie for the rats?" Meg asked between bites of her kabob.

"St. Barnabas. We're going to St. Barnabas. And I haven't seen a rat for days."

Meg had been concerned with rats in the house since I shot one that was hiding under the bed in the loft. I shifted into fourth and turned onto the main road.

"We're going to the church? What for?" she asked, munching away. "I thought we weren't going to the church supper. I just fixed a pretty nice meal."

"Well," I said, trying to break the news gently. "It seems that someone was found dead in the choir loft."

I admit that I have never been good at delivering bad news with a great deal of delicacy, so it was really no surprise that I had to pull over briefly.

"Who?" she whispered, as we cleaned pieces of the chewed onions and green peppers off the inside of the windshield. "Who was it?"

"I don't know," I replied, pulling back onto the road. "Dave didn't know either. He and Nancy are meeting us at the church."

We really do have a lovely, quiet little town up in these North Carolina mountains. It's sort of touristy for those tourists who know about it, but most of them head for Blowing Rock or Boone or even Banner Elk. In the winter months we have plenty of snow, but no ski slopes, so our tourist season happens in the autumn when the colors are at their peak. In October, Mother Nature favors St. Germaine with more adornment than any one town deserves, most of it due to a town ordinance that was ramrodded through a closed council session by the mayor on October 15, 1961 forbidding the cutting of any healthy tree in the downtown area. At the time, the ordinance was viewed as antibusiness and antigrowth, but the $1000 per-tree fine kept most of the old vegetation intact, and since new construction was generally predicated on clearing unused land, most business owners chose to remain in their old buildings and refurbish them—all this at a time when it was much more fashionable to tear everything down and start from scratch. The upshot was that while most small towns were embracing the architectural style of the fifties and sixties, now known as "bad," and eventually losing their downtown areas, St. Germaine remained pretty much as it had for the last hundred years. I might add that there is now a statue of Harrison Sterling, the old mayor, gracing the downtown park. As the plaque says—a man of foresight and wisdom.

The autumn foliage fills the five bed and breakfasts in town every day during the peak season and our one hotel is full from October first through Thanksgiving. The antique shops on Main Street can do enough business to carry them through the rest of the year and you can't even get a table at The Slab. Driving into town from my place is breathtaking in October, especially at sunset, and usually either Megan or I would comment on the view, but on that particular evening we didn't even notice it. In fact, Meg hadn't said a word since I told her the news and that, in itself, was strangely unsettling. I looked over at her. She was sitting very still and staring straight ahead.

We pulled into the church at about 6:45 and I was surprised to see that a crowd had already gathered. Surprised until I remembered that Mother Ryan had planned a church supper and lecture for seven o'clock. The people milling around outside on the front steps were just getting the news. Herself, wearing a gray business suit with a ruffle at the collar, and looking like she was ready for a board meeting, was blocking the door.

"Hayden! Thank God!"

"Thanks for taking charge, Loraine. Say a prayer and send everyone home, will you?"

"No! I can't. I mean, I have a special guest speaker. She has to leave tomorrow morning. She's going to speak on 'Wimmyn's Empowerment in the Ministry.' She's a nationally known author."

"Sorry, Loraine. Send 'em home."

She blocked my way, desperate now.

"Didn't you hear me? She's nationally known. *Nationally known!*"

I turned to face the crowd that had gathered in front of the church. "Friends," I announced. "There has been a death in the church. I don't know yet who it was or if it was an accident or purposeful mischief, but it is my job to find out. I want you all to go home, but before you go, please join me in a word of prayer.

"Our heavenly Father..." I glanced up. Herself was standing next to me shaking with silent rage. "Our Father," I began again, "we know that you have received one of your lambs back into your fold this evening. It grieves us and shocks us but we know you are the same God whose quality it is always to show mercy and whose compassion covers us as a mother hen covers her chicks. Grant us a peaceful sleep that we may rise to love and serve you in all our works. In Jesus' Holy name we pray. Amen."

Amens were heard from the crowd and they began dispersing, quietly talking among themselves.

I turned to Herself. She, I noticed, was beginning to develop quite a twitch. "You can stay if you want," I offered. I swear, I didn't know how that woman had any jaw muscles left at all.

Meg joined me at the door and put her arm around my waist.

Nancy had found the lights by the time we had dispersed the crowd and entered the narthex through the front doors. The steps to the choir loft were directly to the right so we went on up.

St. Barnabas was built in the early 1900's on a classical American design. The nave, or main body of the church, was in the shape of a cross and so named because the ceiling of medieval churches resembled the bottom of a huge boat. Nave meaning "ship" and being the root word of our term "naval." The nautical term, that is—not navel, the umbilical attachment. The transepts, or alcoves, near the front formed the arms of the cross. The high altar was in the front, a smaller Mary altar in the east transept, with the choir and the pipe organ in the back balcony. The sacristy, where the clergy put on their vestments and where communion was prepared, was behind the front wall with two almost invisible doors opening in the paneling behind the altar. It wasn't a large structure. Seating was limited to about two hundred fifty. We only had about one hundred twenty-five communicants, so we were far from full on most Sundays.

Climbing the stairs to the loft, we saw Dave and Nancy bending over a body lying next to the organ.

"What's the verdict?" I asked.

"He's dead all right," Dave offered.

"Maybe he heard Sunday's sermon," I muttered under my breath, perhaps a little too loudly. I looked up. Sure enough, Mother Ryan was glaring at me. I gave her a sheepish grin.

"I don't see any wounds." Nancy squatted and took a closer look. "There doesn't seem to be any bleeding. Should I turn him over?"

Dave reached for the body's shoulder. "Here, let me help you."

Nancy was probably strong enough to turn the body over by herself. She was slim and tall and had a swimmer's upper body strength. I never asked her if she was a competitive swimmer or perhaps a low brass player, but she sure had a trombone player's shoulders. Her uniform, which she always wore while on duty, slightly accentuated her cultivated masculinity. She kept her brown hair fairly short and her figure, from what I could tell, was more boyish than voluptuous. When Dave was around her, though, he was like a lovesick puppy. If the two of them were to arm wrestle for a beer, my money would be on Nancy. Where Nancy looked like a TV cop always ready for business, Dave looked more like Dilbert with an even worse haircut.

They struggled to turn him over. A dead body is always more unwieldy than a living one, but we all already knew who it was. People you're familiar with are identifiable even from the back. It was Willie Boyd, the sexton.

Willie wasn't exactly the likable sort. In fact, most of the parishioners avoided Willie like the plague. As the sexton, he was basically the janitor and was in charge of cleaning the church and locking up after everyone had left. It was a job that he completed mostly at night and the staff left him notes as to what needed doing to avoid personal contact. This arrangement was just fine with the staff because in addition to his abrasive and generally nasty personality, Willie usually smelled of cheap aftershave which he used liberally to disguise his questionable bathing habits, his equally unwashed clothing and the cheap cigar he always had dangling from his sneering lips. He had been the sexton at St. Barnabas for about a year and had been the only applicant for the position that had been advertised for six full months. There weren't a lot of unemployed folks in St. Germaine, and those that were didn't want or need a part-time job as a janitor. Something like a job tended to mess up the unemployment check.

My first thought was that Willie had had a heart attack but my thinking changed once he was rolled onto his back. His eyes were open, and his lips were pulled back from his teeth in a snarl. He had vomited before he died and upon further inspection I noticed that he had lost most of his vittles all over the organ console.

"Jeez," I said. "It might be a heart attack, but I don't think so. Get the coroner and an ambulance down here from Boone. We're gonna need an autopsy. And Nancy, let's scrape whatever crap we can off the keyboard, put it in a plastic bag and send it down with him. I'll have to take the stupid thing apart to clean it before Sunday."

Mother Ryan was standing toward the back of the loft, watching with dispassionate distaste. Megan was closer to the stairs as if she would dart down them at any second.

"Who called it in?" I asked Nancy, who immediately flipped open her notepad in a most officious manner.

"The 911 came up to me from Boone. It was made in by an

unknown caller from the church's number."

"Who was here?" I wondered aloud. "Well, nothing we can do till the coroner arrives," I said. Let's get a cup of coffee in the kitchen."

"I'm leaving," Mother Ryan announced, pushing past Meg. "I still have a guest sitting in the car."

I reached under the organ bench to see if my 9mm was still there. It was. I thought I might be able to wing her before she made the door. Nah.

We went through the sanctuary, into the sacristy, out the back door, down some steps into the alley and into the back door of the kitchen. The parish hall, of which the kitchen was a part, was a separate building with a hallway linking it to the sanctuary from the front but opening to an alley in the back. JJ Southerland was standing by the stove stirring a large pot of soup with a cut off canoe paddle.

"I presume that soup is for the supper tonight?"

"Of course, dahling."

JJ's southern accent is hard to place. It's almost British in its gentility and it is a joy to listen to her. Of course, she's just plain nuts and one of my favorite people. She's been cooking for the church for years. She's not part of the staff, but she enjoys doing what she has time for. Sometimes her soup is delicious. Sometimes it is the worst stuff you ever put in your mouth.

"Your crew isn't coming for supper," I said to JJ as I poured a cup of coffee and handed it to Meg who had come in right behind me.

"I heard. But I might as well finish the soup for Sunday."

"It was Willie."

"Well, I'm sorry," she said, not looking up from her pot, her two hands continuing to pull the paddle though the vegetable-laden hodgepodge.

Dave had gotten a soda out of the machine. I got a cup of coffee for myself and for Nancy. The good thing about the St. Barnabas kitchen was that there was always a cup of coffee and it was always good. Not that weak, watery swill that most churches pass for coffee. St. Barnabas had Community Coffee shipped in monthly from Louisiana. I didn't know if we had a Minister of Coffee or if angels came down and fixed it on a regular basis, but there was always a pot ready to drink. It was sort of like Elijah and the jar of oil that never emptied—an analogy I enjoyed.

Dave walked over and looked into the pot. "Mistake," I thought. JJ didn't like people looking into a pot of unfinished soup.

"What's in it?" Dave asked. "Did you say it was beef?"

"No," said JJ. "Not beef. I said beak. Duck beeeeak."

Dave was an easy mark.

I drank my coffee and turned to JJ. "You didn't make the 911 call, did you?" I was trying to be as offhand and innocuous as possible.

"No, I did not!" said JJ emphatically, glaring at me. "You think I would do that without calling you first?"

"Nah. I guess not." I paused, then framed another question. "I think Willie might have been poisoned. Did he come by here and get anything to eat before he went to work?"

JJ stared daggers at me, pulling up one of the straps on her overalls that had slid down over her shoulder. "I've been here since three. He came by once but didn't take anything. Then I did pass him in the hall on my way to the bathroom. That was about five, I guess. But if he was poisoned, it wasn't anything that *I* cooked!"

"Any food missing?"

"Nothing I brought. I don't know what was in the fridge."

Meg was leaning against the counter, cupping her coffee in both hands as if trying to warm herself over the mug.

"Why would someone do such a thing?" she asked of no one

in particular. Nancy put an arm around her.

The refrigerator was stocked with staples. It was a commercial model of stainless steel with wire racks. I pushed around some sticks of margarine, mayonnaise and other condiments, some leftover Jello salad from last week, some kind of marinade and other unidentifiable but seemingly harmless stuff. I really didn't know what I was looking for.

"Let's empty the refrigerator and send everything down to the lab in Boone. I know it's a pain, but we don't need to take any chances."

I lifted the bowl of marinade and gave it a sniff, but in reality, I didn't have a clue what I was sniffing for. I thought briefly about sticking my finger into the bowl and giving it a taste, but a vision of Willie lying up in the choir loft made me quickly put the bowl back onto the shelf.

Meg found a couple of empty liquor boxes in the corner of the kitchen by the sink and started to empty the refrigerator, glad for something to do. Dave came over from where he was trying to decide if he dared to try some duck-beak soup and began helping her.

"Come on, Nancy," I said. "Let's go wait for the coroner."

Chapter 3

It was a long, quiet twelve miles back to the house.

"I liked your prayer," Meg said finally, breaking the silence and giving me a kiss on the cheek. "The one you gave outside the church. I was afraid for a minute that you were going to do one of your stupid prayers."

I looked offended. "There are no stupid prayers."

"You know...like the one you offered last Thanksgiving at my house, in front of my relatives. If I may I quote you. 'Thank you God for dairy products including cheese and on this, the 26th day of November, we thank you especially for Roquefort, Brie and all the many varieties of cheddar. Thank you God for turkeys who willingly gave their lives that we might celebrate your bounty. Thank you God for grain from which we get our bread and beer. Thank you God for all your many vegetables, especially Raymond Burr. And thank you God for hamsters and all the little things that make our life worth living. Amen.'"

"How could you remember all that? I didn't think your memory was that good."

"I told Mother to record it."

"What!?"

"I told her that she wouldn't believe it, so she had better record it. She wrote it down afterwards for posterity. And possibly blackmail."

"I'm glad to have made her life a little brighter."

"Well" she sniffed, "she was not amused. She takes Thanksgiving rituals very seriously. And Raymond Burr's been dead for years."

"He was the only vegetable I could think of on the spur of the moment."

"You're supposed to be a man of the church."

Actually Meg's mother seemed to like me a lot. Although she'd wanted Megan to meet me, I doubt that she originally viewed me as son-in-law material. I'm sure Meg changed her mind by casually dropping some information about my portfolio along the way.

The silence broken, we wound our way through the mountains, making small talk and managing somehow to dance delicately around the looming hippopotamus named Willie, until we finally saw the cabin lights we had left burning in our hasty departure. Over the years, Meg has learned to let me ponder for a while before drawing me into speculation about a case. We pulled into the drive, turned off the truck and went back through the kitchen door.

My cabin is situated on about two hundred acres about twelve miles from town. It included some good bottom land that was originally used to grow tobacco, several mountains and a good sized creek winding through the whole thing. I call it a "cabin" because one of the rooms—now my office—is a twenty-by-twenty log cabin with a loft that was originally built in 1842. I bought it from a fellow in eastern Kentucky who swore he had documentation that the cabin was built by Daniel Boone's granddaughter. I'm not sure I believed him, but the cabin was in great shape, having been covered with clapboards for the last hundred years, and it came with a good story. We numbered the logs, took it apart and moved it to North Carolina. The rest of the rather large house was built to complement it. It sported a huge stone fireplace, a stuffed elk head above the mantle, and a lot of leather furniture. It suited me just fine.

I grabbed a beer and I sat back down at the typewriter, hoping that a little imaginative prose would help clear my thoughts.

"I heard about the hymn selection last Sunday."

Her voice was low as she stood in front of me, filling out a brown tweed suit the way Reggie White filled out the Packers' front line. Usually I didn't care for tweed on women. I was more of a chiffon and lace kind of guy. And this was that rough kind of tweed that you could strike a match on. So I did. She didn't flinch.

"Just for the record," she growled, "I don't think you did it. You just don't look like the kind of guy who would schedule 'Just As I Am' as a processional."

You know, I didn't like her attitude. She was taking far more for granted than I thought she should. I lit my cigar.

"Maybe I did pick it. Maybe I really think that 'Just As I Am' has a regal majesty combined with just a hint of pietism that makes it the perfect processional hymn for the Twenty-fourth Sunday after Pentecost."

Laughter escaped her lips as she picked up an open hymnal lying on the desk. I had left it open to "Hyfrydol" with the date penciled in beside the title. Rats.

"OK," I said, grabbing the book from her hand and throwing it back into the corner with all the other denominational hymnals. "Just what is it you want?"

Pulling up a chair, she sat down gracefully, crossing her tweed-covered legs with an elegance belying the sound of tweed-on-tweed, a sound not unlike forty Amish farmers shucking corn. "I heard you were good with altos and I need some advice. My name is Denver. Denver Tweed."

They were always coming to me for advice. I had gotten a reputation over the years. A reputation as a tough but understanding guy. It was a reputation I didn't deserve. I was in it for the money.

"It'll cost you."

I could tell she wasn't put off a bit as she dropped two C-notes on the desk in front of me and pulled a meerschaum pipe from her pocket. Somehow I wasn't surprised. Tweed and meerschaum. What next?

"Someone stole my elbow patches."

Like I said before, I wasn't surprised.

On Saturday morning, Meg and I trucked our way back to St. Barnabas to meet with my two cohorts and clean up the choir loft. Nancy, Dave and I scraped some more samples indicative of Willie's demise, bagged them, and looked around again for any obvious clues. Finding none, Dave and Nancy left Megan and me to the arduous task of making the church presentable.

Meg had brought enough cleaning supplies to purify the entire church. The only time I had seen her more determined, janitorially speaking, is after I shot that rat under the bed. She scrubbed that bedroom from top to bottom.

In my defense, I actually tried to hit the rat before it made cover, but it kept running up the log walls and I figured, and rightfully so, that a few more bullet holes would only enhance the look of the old timbers. Still, all good things must come to an end and when Mr. Rattus Norvegicus stopped to catch his breath, Mr. Remington was happy to make his acquaintance. Meg was appalled at the entire episode, even after I pointed out that rats were a fact of life in the woods and being shot was a much quicker and more humane death than being poisoned.

"I don't see how getting shot is better."

"Poison takes longer. And then the rats die in the walls or behind the refrigerator."

"What about a trap?"

"I've got some set out back in the shed, but sometimes it takes days to catch them. Perhaps I should go with a 'live and let live' policy. Of course you never know where they'll show up. The shower...the dresser drawer..."

"No," she said with an involuntary shiver. "Shoot them."

We spent the better part of three hours in the choir loft. I opened the console of the organ, lifted out each key, cleaned it and made sure the mechanics were unaffected. It was mostly superficial cleanup though. Nothing that I could see had gotten into the works.

Meg cleaned the floor and the chairs—everything that had an actual surface that she could wipe down. When we were finished, we grabbed a couple sandwiches from The Slab and spent a long, lazy Saturday afternoon at the cabin doing not much of anything that I can discuss without being thought of as a cad.

Around six o'clock Meg took off to her own hacienda to re-charge and to check on her mother. I took out a pad and pen and began to take some notes.

When?

Willie Boyd was killed on Friday. Late afternoon. JJ had seen him around five. She was the last to see him, other than maybe the killer. Did that make JJ a suspect? Probably. She was the only one in the church that I know about, except for the person who called 911. I'd get a tape of that call from Boone on Monday.

Who?

Someone who knew him? Probably.

Why?

Willie didn't have any enemies that I was aware of yet. He kept to himself and did his job. In November and December he also worked at the Grandfather Mountain Tree Farm selling Christmas trees. Herself did make a complaint about Willie to the vestry, claiming sexual harassment about three weeks ago. But how much of that was true? I would check on this next week.

How?

I suspected that he was probably poisoned. We'd have the lab report back on Tuesday.

What?

What?! Who came up with the five-question rule anyway? It's a stupid question.

I felt brilliant.

The Sunday service went surprisingly smoothly after our trag-edy and I noticed that Nancy was back in the congregation. Some-times she shows up when she's feeling low. When her boyfriend left town, she was at St. Barnabas for five Sundays in a row, joined a Sunday School, got baptized, and started a prayer group. She hadn't been too regular since then, but she made one or two appearances a month.

Maybe the murder had taken the edge off Mother Ryan for a few days. Hope springs eternal. The choir sang *The Eyes of All* by Charles Wood at the offertory and sang it very well. Communion, though, was a bit harried. The wine, which was always brought from the sacristy, was late. In fact, the *Agnus Dei* had already begun when one of the lay eucharistic ministers finally returned with the cup. I thought it was a bit odd. I expected such shenanigans from Mother Ryan, but I knew the LEMs were trained better than that.

Agnus Dei, qui tolis peccata mundi,
miserere nobis.
Lamb of God, who takes away the sins of the world,
Have mercy upon us.

We finished communion and followed the sacrament with the final hymn. Complete with a stunning harmonization on the last stanza written by yours truly—including a soprano descant.

The tradition of St. Barnabas was to meet for coffee and donuts in the parish hall right after services. It was a time for the congregation to "meet, greet and eat" as it was advertised in the bulletin. I said hello to Nancy and left her talking to Meg while I pigeonholed Georgia Wester, one of the servers.

"What was the deal this morning?" I asked her, disgust evident in my voice. Herself usually managed to get something wrong and it was, as I put it, "a constant grain of sand in my otherwise pearl-less oyster." Meg pointed out that I should be glad of a pearl and the irritation was just part of the process. I replied that it was never the oyster who enjoyed the pearl.

"It wasn't her fault this time," Georgia explained. "It was mine. I was late this morning. I thought Bev had prepared communion.

She thought I had. It wouldn't have been a problem except that when I went back to get it during the offertory, the bottle was gone. I went into the kitchen, looked in the closet for another bottle and the *closet* was empty. I had to drive down the street and get a couple of bottles from The Slab."

"The Slab? For communion wine?"

Georgia smiled. "You just have to know who to ask."

"Let's look in the wine closet," I suggested.

Georgia shrugged. I motioned Nancy over and Georgia led us through the kitchen to the back closet. It was an old door, made of oak panels and probably original to the building. She pulled a set of keys out of her pocket and inserted an old skeleton key into the lock.

"It always sticks," she grumbled, giving it a shake or two and trying to get notches of the key to slip into the tumblers. After a moment's work, the key turned stiffly in the lock and the door swung open. She was right. It was empty.

She pointed to the vacant shelves. "There should be three cases at least. Twenty-four or twenty-five bottles."

"Do we always use two bottles per service?" I asked.

"We usually have a magnum, so we just need one. But The Slab didn't have any magnums."

"Jeez," I said, mumbling to myself. "Jeez, the wine—."

Meg was chatting with some other choir members and finishing up her coffee. I got her attention.

"I think it was the communion wine. Let's go back to the loft." All four of us, Meg, Nancy, Georgia and I, headed out the kitchen door, back into the church and made our way up into the loft.

I instructed the troops. "We're looking for a wine bottle. A big one. Megan, you and Georgia look up around the chairs over by the window. Nancy, let's you and I look down here by the rail. If you find it, don't touch it."

"Hayden, we already cleaned this place from top to bottom." Meg offered.

"We didn't know what we were looking for."

I figured that if the bottle was up here, Willie probably would have hidden it for later consumption. I had a hard time believing that even Willie would have finished an entire magnum bottle in the two hours he was out of sight. He probably had stashed it somewhere.

Nancy was the first to sing out. "Hey boss. There's a loaded 9mm Glock here under the organ bench."

"Don't worry about it. It's mine."

I looked up at Meg in time to see her roll her eyes and drop her head into her hands. But she was always overreacting.

Georgia was next. "Hey, there's an empty flask in the hymnal rack over here."

"Nah. That's Marjorie's. Keep looking." Marjorie was known to take a snort or two during services.

I myself was looking in the organ pipe case on the opposite side of the loft. It had a swing-out door for tuning the instrument and anything hidden inside would be fairly accessible yet easily hidden. I thought for sure that's where I'd find the bottle. I saved this little hiding place for myself, of course, so I could find the bottle in front of everyone and impress Meg with my deductive prowess.

It didn't work. Nancy called out "Got it!" and my plan for self-glorification was toast.

She had found the offending bottle in the bell tower. Actually there was a small room, which was usually kept locked, directly off the loft. It was this room that held the ladder that led directly up another flight and a half to the church bell. The rest of the stuff in the room was junk. There was an old sound system consisting of some old amps and an 8-track, old 1940 hymnals and 1928 prayer books, some shelves, old paint cans. The usual stuff. I had assumed the door was still locked. It wasn't, and of course Willie had the key. The bottle was placed just as nicely as you please on one of the shelves. There was a corkscrew, obviously purloined from the kitchen, lying next to the bottle and his half-smoked cigar placed neatly on the shelf, the inch long ash hanging over the edge of the discolored wooden board. Next to the cigar was a green matchbook that was embossed with "Pine Valley Christmas Tree Farm" in bright red letters. I opened it and noticed that there were three matches gone. We were lucky that Willie smoked cheap cigars. An expensive brand would have kept burning and probably ignited the entire church. As it was, Willie's twenty-five cent cigars had to be puffed on pretty heavily to remain lit. When he set it down to pour his drink and didn't pick it back up, the cigar—luckily—had burned out. The cork to the wine bottle was halfway out or, if my suspicions were correct, halfway back in.

"Oh man," I said, suddenly remembering everything I had forgotten to bring with me. "Nancy, did you bring any gloves? Mine are in the truck."

"Right here, boss," she said, producing a box of physician's disposable latex wear and a baggie from her purse.

"What a babe!" I said. Then, remembering my PC rules, quickly changed to "I mean, thank you Officer."

Nancy snorted in good-natured disgust and handed me the box.

I pulled out a pair of gloves and snapped them on. Holding the bottle up to the light given off by the single bulb, it was easy to see that Mssr. Willie had taken quite a swig before putting the bottle on the shelf. I handed it to Nancy who had donned gloves of her own. Then I bagged the cigar and dropped it into my pocket along with the matchbook.

"Voilá!" I said. "As Archimedes so eloquently put it as he ran naked through the streets of Athens, 'Eureka! Eureka!'"

"What do you mean, 'You found it?' I found it!" Nancy retorted, glaring at me.

"And I didn't know you spoke Greek," I said in surprise.

"Everyone knows what 'eureka' means."

"I suppose so. Anyway, you get full credit. Make sure you mention yourself kindly when you type up the report tomorrow."

"Gee, thanks, boss."

Chapter 4

"I know you're not here for your elbow patches." I laughed and lit a cigar. It was a full-throated laugh and I could see it was driving her crazy.

Her eyes were smoldering--smoldering as the passion that hung heavy in the room like some gigantic velvet curtain smothering the atmosphere that rose like the thin wisp of smoke from the extinguished match she had just used to light a cigar of her own.

"That is the worst sentence I ever been involved in," she said, disgust evident in her voice.

"Evidently, you've never read me before."

Yeah, I've seen a million of 'em and they were all alike. Unemployed English majors.

She was attractive in the sort of way that some heavy women with very short hair and no makeup, wearing a three piece brown-tweed suit with wingtips and smoking a cigar can be called attractive. She reminded me of my Aunt Mable. Or Winston Churchill.

"All right," she hissed, leaning over the desk, smoke escaping through her clenched teeth like the angry breath of some ancient pope. "Let's get to the point."

"What's your hurry?" I said, puffing smoke of my own right back in her face. "We've got plenty of time." It wasn't easy talking and puffing at the same time, but I had to show her I was every bit the man she was. And she was getting steamed. As steamed as last night's clams.

"This chapter's half over thanks to your insipid metaphors. And if you want any semblance of a plot, not to mention character development, you'd better get moving."

She was really ranting now. I could always tell when they were mad. This one was beet-red and her hands were clenching and unclenching the loaded shotgun that I had left sitting on the table. I suddenly realized I had made a tactical error. Still, I had her hooked like a tweed tuna and I had to reel her in. "These ain't metaphors. Only an idiot would try to use an unlicensed metaphor in a detective story. These what I'm usin' is similes pure and simple." I lit a cigar.

I thought it was ingenious, cloaking my superior knowledge in bad grammar to point up the ridiculousness of her statement. I even smiled as I saw the shotgun come up in slow motion. She was mad as a wet bishop and I had her right where I wanted her. Suddenly there was a knock on the door and Cecil, my sandwich delivery boy, burst in with my lunch.

Monday I slept late. I had given Nancy the bottle we'd found to take down to the lab in Boone so I figured that I had a slow morning coming. The phone started ringing just as I was wandering into the kitchen scratching places that men only scratch if there are no women in the house. I picked up the phone and clicked the ringer to "mute" at the same time I answered.

"Konig," I said brusquely.

"Hayden, it's almost 10:30. When're you coming in."

I recognized Nancy's voice through my pre-caffeinated haze. "What's up?"

"We've been waiting for you. You've got to hear this."

"What is it?" I asked, now definitely awake. Nancy wouldn't call unless it was important and now she had definitely stirred my interest.

"It's a call that came into the station at 5:10 on Friday. Wanna hear it?"

"Can you play it over the phone?"

"You bet. Hang on a second."

There was a pause—then I heard Dave's dulcet baritone. "You've reached the St. Germaine Police Department. There is no one here to take your call. If it is an emergency, hang up and dial 911. Your call will be forwarded. Otherwise, please leave a message."

I thought it sounded very professional. Just the way I wrote it.

There was a pause on the tape, then a long beep and then a voice.

"This here's Willie Boyd up at St. Barnabas Church. There's been a break-in. I don't guess it's no emergency, but all the wine is missing from the closet in the kitchen. Prob'ly three cases. I done fixed the lock on the closet door already. Thank you for your time." Click.

Nancy came back on. "Did you get that?"

"Well, Casper the Holy Ghost!" I exclaimed. "What time did you say that call came in?"

"5:10."

"So he was still alive at that point. What time was the 911 call?"

"We just got that from Boone. I sent Dave to get it at seven this morning. He took the bottle and the rest of the stuff down, too."

"Have you listened to it?"

"Yep. It's just a copy. They wouldn't give us the real tape. It's a woman's voice. It's familiar but I can't place it. They record these calls so slowly it's hard to recognize a particular voice sometimes. The time is 5:17 p.m."

"Can you play it for me?"

"Nope. The answering machine is digital, but this is a cassette and the only cassette player is in your office. I can play it over the phone, but you might as well just come in."

"Man." I paused, doing the math. "That narrows it down to seven minutes."

"Yep." Nancy sounded almost perky. "He drank the poison sometime between 5:10 and 5:17."

"Do we know it was poison? Is the lab report back?"

48

"Sorry. I was just guessing."

"I'll be there before noon. Hold down the fort."

I put some coffee in the drip machine. I have an espresso machine too—one of my nods towards my ever-dwindling stock fortune—but I didn't have time to fool with it this morning and besides, I needed to think.

I showered quickly and chose my green flannel shirt and chinos as my ensemble of the day. When you only have one shirt and one pair of pants that are clean, it's a pretty easy choice. I picked up a load of laundry, threw it in the washing machine and set them happily gyrating as I headed back to the kitchen for my coffee. Then I called Georgia Wester, who had prepared the altar for Sunday's service. She answered on the second ring.

"Hi Georgia. Hayden. Listen, did you get the bread and wine ready for communion on Saturday like you usually do?"

"Nope. I knew I would be gone on Saturday so I did it on Friday before lunch."

"So you had a bottle of wine on the counter in the sacristy?"

"Yes."

"Thanks."

"That's all?"

"That's all. Bye."

I got my list off the refrigerator and checked it over. Basically nothing new here except the time of death and the wine theft. I made some notes and shoved the list in my pocket. Maybe I could recognize the voice on the 911 tape. I had a better ear than Nancy and I knew most of the people in the congregation. I poured a large cup of coffee into a traveling mug and got into my old blue chariot, popping in a Wynton Marsalis *Baroque Music for Trumpets* CD. I had one stop to make before I got into town. The McCollough's trailer.

The McCollough's place was about halfway between my spread and town, up in the hills and hard to find. Ardine McCollough lived with her three children in a 1972 vintage mobile home that was definitely showing its age. I don't know what happened to Ardine's husband, PeeDee. According to local legend, he just disappeared one day. I suspect he simply took off, but the rumor whispered around town was that he had been murdered by Ardine and buried somewhere down in the holler. Ardine never filed a missing persons report and I didn't put any stock in the rumors, so I never bothered to investigate. He'd been gone for five years, leaving when the youngest child was still a baby. PeeDee was a physically abusive son-of-a-bitch with a penchant for drinking coupled with a quick temper. I had been out to their trailer to have a few serious chats with him—once, after Ardine had checked into the emergency room in Boone. I had even locked him up once, but Ardine declined to press charges and he was out in twenty-four hours, sober as a judge and promising never to do it again. I had heard through the town grapevine that he had started taking his frustrations out on Bud, the oldest child, but I hadn't seen any evidence of it firsthand. All this considered, it was my feeling that if Ardine truly had done what it was rumored she'd done, then I figured she had to live with it.

One thing the man *did* do before he left, was name his children after beer. The oldest boy, Bud, was fourteen, and he was the one that had been caught stealing wine all over town last year. Name-wise, he was a lucky one, because the shortened version of Budweiser at least resembled a common name. The second child was named Pauli Girl. She was twelve. The youngest was a cute six-year old boy named Moose-Head—Moosey for short.

Moosey greeted me as I drove up the dirt drive to the trailer. He was playing in a rock pile, heaving stones bigger than his head down a ravine beside the drive.

"Hayden!" he yelled as I pulled up. He dropped the rock he had balanced over his head and met me as I stepped out of my truck with a bear hug around both my legs.

"Let go, Moosey. If I fall, we'll break at least three legs. Why aren't you in school?"

"Teacher's workday." He was laughing and going through my pockets, looking for the candy bar I almost always brought him.

"Where is it?" he asked, looking very disappointed when he didn't find anything.

"Sorry, I forgot. Tell you what. I'll drop by on the way home and bring you something good. How's that?"

He was placated immediately and resumed rearranging the rock pile.

Ardine was standing on the porch. She had her hands crossed in front of her very defensively, her elbows tucked into her sides and a scowl on her face as if she expected the worst. She was wearing a cotton dress that she had probably made herself, just as she made most of their clothes. Her graying hair was pulled into a loose ponytail. Over her dress was an old cardigan sweater, several sizes too large, making her appear even smaller and more bird-like than she was. Her face was thin and lined and she might once have been very pretty. Now in her early forties, she had the look of someone who had lived a hard life. Her right eye had a slight droop and didn't close all the way when she blinked, which she did often, thanks chiefly to the nerve damage that PeeDee had inflicted upon it with a left hook after a night of drinking. I had rarely seen her smile. She worked at a nearby Christmas tree farm. I had no doubt that it was hard, manual labor and that she actually brought home less money than she would with the state's unemployment check.

I went up the steps to the porch.

"Get to it," she said quietly, chewing on her lower lip.

"Ardine, I just need to ask Bud a couple of questions. Don't get upset."

"What's he done now?"

"I don't know that he's done anything. I just need to ask him a few things. He hasn't been in trouble since last year has he?"

"No."

51

"And he wasn't in trouble before that, was he?"

"No."

"Then it's probably nothing. But I do need to talk to him."

Her shoulders slumped and she looked resigned to whatever was coming. "C'mon in then."

I went in the front door, sat down on the sofa. I looked around the trailer which was, as always, as neat as Matilda's hat-pin. Ardine had made the curtains, the slipcovers, the quilts—everything—from castoffs and free remnants she got at the fabric store in Boone. It was a deal that I put together for her. I know the owner.

Bud came in and sat down across from me. His back straight as a ramrod. He was scared. Bud was a nice, polite kid. Not the usual kid with a chip on his shoulder that came out of these hills. He had a library card and he used it almost daily. He was fourteen and had been driving the old truck since he was eleven, but we never bothered him.

"How're you doing, Bud?" I asked him.

"Fine, sir," he said, his voice quivering.

"You know why I'm here?"

"No, sir," he answered softly.

"Someone broke into St. Barnabas on Friday afternoon and stole some wine. Would you know anything about that?"

Ardine broke in. "He was here with me all day Friday. He didn't even take the truck into town."

"It's true! I didn't!" exclaimed Bud. "I wouldn't take wine from the church anyway."

"Why not?"

"It's awful stuff. You see, communion wine doesn't have to taste good. It can be just about any red wine and usually is whatever's on sale. You can get a magnum for under ten dollars. It was probably a Muscadet or something from Mogen-David.

"If I was going to *steal* anything," he went on, "I'd be looking for a Châteauneuf-du-Pape, although the taste is probably no better than a lot of burgundies or a good Spanish Rojas. I'd sort of like to have one though. Pouilly-Fuissé is a pretty good dry and fruity white Burgundy, but what I'd really be after is a Cabernet Savignon or a Zinfandel from Mayacamas. Mayacamas is a California winery and their wine is supposed to be really excellent. I wouldn't even mind a bottle of Stag's Leap Chardonnay. The wine is supposed to be pretty good, but I just really like the name, don't you? You know, Gallo has a Chenin Blanc which has been knocking off premium wineries in comparative tastings, but I just have a real problem with any wine that has Gallo on the label."

The words tumbled from his mouth in an enthusiastic rush. I'm pretty sure my mouth was hanging open. I looked at Ardine. She was just as bewildered as I was.

"I'd also like to get hold of a Domaine Roux Père et Fils from St. Aubin. Apparently, their wine can hold its own in blind tastings with a lot of other Meursaults. Or a Château de Rodet from the village of Rully. I'm really hooked on the white burgundies. They're both fairly inexpensive now and guaranteed to go up in price."

Bud's French was far from flawless, most of it picked up from books, and my hand moved to my mouth to cover my smile.

"Do you...drink a lot of wine?" I asked.

"No sir," he said, looking me in the eye for the first time since our interview started. "I'm only fourteen. I'm not allowed to drink."

I had to ask. "Bud, why did you steal those bottles of wine last year?"

"Well," he said, as though he didn't know whether to confide in me or not.

"Well, I thought I might go ahead start my cellar. You know, so that when I reached twenty-one, I'd already have a good start. I didn't take very expensive bottles. And they always had a lot more."

"Where did you learn all this stuff?"

"At the library."

As I stood up, I felt a tug at my arm. It was Pauli Girl. "That boy jest ain't right. We all knows it."

"Bud?" I asked. "You don't have to let me, but would you mind if I looked in your room?"

"I don't mind. Is it OK, Mom?"

Ardine was still nervous. "I guess," she said.

We walked down the narrow hallway to Bud and Moosey's room. I reached over Moosey's bed, which was closest to the door, and flipped on the reading light. Then, with Bud and Ardine standing in the doorway watching me, I looked around the boys' bedroom quickly and not a little self-consciously. I flipped on the little flashlight I had pocketed in the truck and flashed it up into the closet, then bent down and looked under the bed. Finally, I opened the dresser drawers finishing my mock-search. I was pretty sure I wouldn't find anything. I was trying for some sort of initial reaction to my search question, but Bud's face was an open book, and if he was lying, it would be easy to tell. He wasn't lying. I turned off the flashlight and reached back across the bed to flip off the light when something on the bedtable caught my eye.

"What's this?" I asked Bud, picking up an old skeleton key, dark brown with age and well used. It had been pushed behind the lamp on the table.

Bud looked at me blankly. "It's a key, I guess. But it's not mine."

I held it up and looked at it more closely. I suspected that I had seen this key, or its twin, in the last twenty-four hours.

"Ardine?"

"Not mine," she said quietly. "Maybe Moosey found it. You can take it if you want."

"Thanks," I said, pocketing the key and giving them a smile. "Anyway, I've got to go."

"Hey, one other thing," Bud said, following me down the hall. "I shouldn't be the one telling, but there's some stuff missing from our trailer."

"Hush now," said Ardine. "Ain't nothin'."

Ardine was still nervous as she followed me onto the porch.

"So, is Bud in trouble?"

"I don't think so. I'll let you know if something else comes up."

"Thanks, Hayden."

I spotted a quilt she was making on the table by the bedroom door. It was a patchwork job in a wedding ring pattern and very nicely done. It would look great in the guest bedroom. Ardine did her quilting after the kids were in bed

"Ardine, would you sell me that quilt?"

She was taken aback.

"I guess so. It's almost finished."

"I don't want to take advantage of you," I said. "How about seven hundred?"

"Seven hundred?" she said, blinking twice.

"OK, eight," I said, reaching into my pocket and peeling off eight hundred dollar bills. "But I want it ready by the time I get back here this afternoon."

I liked to drive a hard bargain.

I got to the station at about 11:30. Nancy was going over a fax with Dave as I walked in.

"What'chugot?" I asked, my accent still holding over from my visit with the McColloughs.

"Lab report. At least the prelim. It was poison all right, but guess what?"

"OK, tell me."

"Not from the wine."

I must admit, I was astonished.

"What do you mean, it wasn't the wine?"

"The residual wine in Willie's stomach showed no poison. They tested the bottle we found. Nothing there either."

"So what was it?"

Nancy was doing her best to read and answer my questions at the same time. "Unknown toxins found in the blood. They're sending it to Chapel Hill for further analysis."

"Oh, that's just great!" I said, my disgust evident. "That'll take about a month."

"I'm afraid so," replied Nancy. "In the meantime they want to know what you want to do with the body."

"Is there a next of kin?"

"Not that we've found."

"Well, let's put him on ice for a week or so. We may need him later when we know what we're looking for."

Nancy nodded. "I'll fax them back."

"Where's the 911 tape?"

"On your desk, Boss," Dave answered.

I went in and dropped the tape in my office stereo. There was the usual 911 identification, then a woman's voice.

"I'd like to report a dead man. He's in the choir loft at St. Barnabas Church in St. Germaine." Click.

The operator tried to get some additional information, but the connection was broken.

Not much, but I thought I detected something about the voice. Whoever she was, she'd tried to hide her identity. It was obviously someone I knew; someone who had a reason to be in the church. I recognized the timbre—it was a familiar voice. I had a feeling I'd connect it with the owner eventually—maybe when I heard it again, but right now I was drawing a blank.

The rest of the day was pretty leisurely. Later that afternoon Mrs. McCarty called because her hedgehogs had gotten loose again and she wanted someone to come over and help her round them up. She sold them to pet stores all over the country and, until the first hard freeze, they were in a pen in the back yard. Unfortunately for her business prospects, the little rascals were always climbing or digging their way out. Once they did, they were pretty

56

much goners. They couldn't survive the winter even if they did survive the summer lawn mowers.

"Mrs. McCarty, this is the police department. We're very busy. We can't come out to help you catch your hedgehogs," Nancy explained nicely for the fifth time this month. It was my plan to get out of the office before Mrs. McCarty demanded to speak to me. I heard Nancy call my name just as the door hit me in the rear.

Later that afternoon, I dropped by the McCollough's to pick up my quilt and give Moosey a box of Jujubes. Then I headed for home.

Chapter 5

It was the best of times, it was the worst of times--the best of times because I was sitting at my desk looking directly at a hot Reuben with melted Swiss cheese creeping out around the edges of fresh rye bread and across the corned beef and sauerkraut like the magma of an unseen volcanic smorgasbord--a sandwich that my Lutheran friend and confidant, Pastor Langknecht, never failed to remind me had won the Grand Prix at the International Sandwich Exposition of 1956 and that, looking at it now, reminded me of an old hymn, "Melt me, mold me, fill me, use me"--the worst of times because a deranged alto, Denver Tweed to be exact, was leveling a shotgun right at my midsection, making my stomache grumble for reasons wholly unrelated to the edible work of art in front of me which, I noticed, was developing quite a grease spot--I wouldn't have to put lemon oil on the desk for years.

This alto, tweedily dressed, wasn't here for her elbow patches.

"Go ahead and eat your sandwich. It will be your last meal."

She clenched the cigar between her teeth, apparently in no hurry to finish me. I suspected there was a reason.

"That's a pretty disgusting opening sentence," Meg said. "I think you should send it in to the Bulwar-Lytton Competition. 'It was a dark and gloomy Sunday.'"

"My quest is not the quest for glory," I said nobly. "I simply want to tell my story."

"Speaking of which," said Meg, "When does the choir get to see this masterpiece?"

"The first installment goes into the choir folders on Sunday morning. I would have put it in last Sunday, but it would probably have been in bad taste."

"I think it's in bad taste for any Sunday." She quickly left the room—not exactly running, but fast enough to avoid the sofa cushion I flung at her.

My pager went off on Thursday afternoon at about five. I called down to the station and Dave answered.

"Better meet Nancy out on Old Chambers Road. About a mile south of town. There's been an accident."

"Anyone we know?" I asked.

"Darlene Puckett. I'm pretty sure she's dead."

"Jeez. Did you call the ambulance?"

"Yes, but they're on another run. They'll be here as soon as they can. From what I gather, there's no real hurry. Her husband called from his cell phone."

"So he's all right?"

"Apparently."

"I'll be there in fifteen minutes."

I pulled up to the scene eighteen minutes after I received the call. There was a car and an old pickup truck pulled over on the side of the road. Old Chambers Road was a torturous, serpentine path leading down the mountain. It didn't get much use since the highway went in, although it had been repaved about thirty years ago. The top speed at which a competent driver could safely navigate Old Chambers was about forty miles per hour and it was well posted. I figured that Darlene had exceeded that directive as she had in so many other locations.

The ambulance was in the middle of the road, lights flashing. Mike and Joe, our regular EMTs, were putting Darlene into the back doors on a stretcher. Luckily there were no cars backed up.

"Our other run was a false alarm," said Joe. "We got here pretty quick."

"We'll take her to the coroner," said Mike. "Nothing we can do. Her name's Darlene Puckett. That's her husband Carlton still sitting in the car."

I nodded. "I know them both."

Joe shook his head. "Her husband said she jumped out of the sunroof. Damnedest thing I ever heard of."

Mike, never at a loss for words, chimed in "She hit the road like a Hefty bag filled with vegetable soup."

I was always amazed at the elegant and poetic comments of our two EMTs.

"Did you pronounce her?" I asked to affirmative nods. "Go ahead and give me the paperwork. I'll fill it out downtown."

As I looked over the clipboard full of documents, Nancy pulled up in our one police vehicle, blue lights flashing and siren set on stun. She parked the car behind the ambulance, cut the siren but left the lights flashing and walked over to where we were discussing the unfortunate Mrs. Puckett.

"She's dead?" Nancy asked, pretty sure of the answer since she was lifting the sheet off Darlene's face even as she asked. "Man, she's pretty beat-up."

"She is definitely the ex-Mrs. Puckett," said Mike.

Joe closed the doors on the ambulance. "Well, let's get her to the morgue. I've got a date at seven."

Mike and Joe pulled away and cut the flashing lights on the ambulance as Nancy and I went to talk with Carlton.

Carlton was still in his Honda Accord, the door open and his feet placed solidly on terra firma where he seemed to be studying his Hush Puppies with great intensity.

"I was going too fast," said Carlton, not looking up as we approached.

"I'm sorry for your loss," said Nancy, pulling her omnipresent "parchment and quill" from her breast pocket. "I know it's a bad time, but can you tell us what happened?"

"She started screaming 'He's back, He's back.' Then she

climbed right out of the sunroof and jumped out of the car."

"Excuse me?" Nancy stopped writing, raised an eyebrow and looked Carlton in the face.

"She thought it was the Rapture," Carlton continued, shaking his head. "You know, like in those *Left Behind* books. She thought Jesus was going to lift her up into the sky. Look, I was trying to slow down, but she wouldn't wait till I stopped."

"Why would she think it was the Rapture?" I asked.

"We passed a half-dozen naked people floating into the air and then she saw Jesus."

"She saw Jesus?" Nancy asked, pen poised over the paper but seemingly unable to take any notes.

"Well," said Carlton, gesturing toward the pickup truck, "anyway, she saw Arlen."

Arlen Pearl was dressed in a white sheet leaning against his old pickup. He was in his mid-thirties I'd guess, but I didn't know for sure. He had shoulder length blonde hair and a beard but, in my opinion, he didn't bear much resemblance to Jesus. Maybe he looked holier from the passenger seat of a car traveling down Old Chambers at forty miles an hour. I gestured him over to the Honda. He came down the road toward us, a hangdog look on his face.

"I shore am sorry, Carlton. I never meant for nothin' like this to happen."

Carlton shook his head in the affirmative but didn't say anything.

"Arlen, what on earth happened?" I asked. "Why are you wearing a sheet? Is there a Klan meeting somewhere I should know about?"

"There ain't no Klan meetin'," he said, shaking his head. "I was goin' to Jimmy Horton's bachelor party. We was s'posed to dress in togas." He stopped.

"And?" I said, trying not to sound impatient. Arlen was straight out of the hollers of North Carolina and would get around to his story in his own time. He had never been in trouble as far as I knew and the only legal advice I ever gave to Arlen was that "if you get married in Western North Carolina and later divorced in West Virginia, remember—she is still legally your sister." He didn't see the humor in it.

Arlen shrugged, and sighed audibly. "OK. I bought eight sex dolls from a catalog and filled them up with helium. They were decorations for Jimmy's party. I was taking them to town in my truck when the tarp came loose. All eight of them took off into the air."

I glanced at Nancy. She looked as though she couldn't even blink much less take notes.

"Then what?" I asked. I was getting a little tired of trying to pull the story out of Arlen.

"I stopped the truck by the side of the road and I was shouting at the dolls 'Come back here.' I guess my arms were up in the air like this," he said, lifting his hands toward the heavens. "I just wanted them to come back. Sheesh. They cost almost thirty dollars apiece. I was going to sell them to the guys after the party. Then Carlton comes racin' by and Darlene jumps out of the sunroof."

Arlen stopped talking and paused for a moment. "That's it. I never 'spected nothin' like this to happen."

Carlton looked up. "She just loved Jesus so much. And I was going too fast to stop."

"I know she loved him, Carlton." I said.

Carlton looked off into the distance. "The last thing I said to her was I thought she smelled like wisteria." He looked at me with a sad smile. "I read it in a book."

"They all smell like that," said Arlen. "It's this perfume they put on."

Nancy and I walked back to her car.

"Is that the weirdest thing you've ever heard of?" she asked.

"Nah. There was a guy in Los Angeles a couple of years ago

who drowned in his bathtub while he was trying to learn to walk on water."

"Huh?"

"Seems like he slipped on a bar of soap and knocked himself out when he cracked his head. His wife found him about an hour later."

"Is that true?"

"Don't know," I said. "But it's a good story."

Over a week had passed since Willie Boyd was found and we were still waiting for the lab report to come back from Chapel Hill. I had an appointment with Herself and the vestry at four o'clock to get some official information about the sexual harassment complaint that Loraine had lodged against Willie.

I drove up to St. Barnabas with the Mozart *Coronation Mass* blaring on the stereo and the windows rolled down. We were having a snap of Indian Summer and I was enjoying the unseasonably warm weather. I pulled into the parking lot just as Malcolm Walker and his wife, Rhiza, were getting out of his jade-colored Beemer. Malcolm, the Senior Warden, was in charge of the vestry, the church's financial dealings, and had his finger on the pulse of St. Barnabas. Rhiza was also on the vestry and a member of the Altar Guild, but she didn't say much during the meetings. She always voted with Malcolm, much to the chagrin of some of the other members, but I knew that there was more substantive gray matter behind Rhiza's beautiful blue eyes than she wanted anyone to believe. Malcolm was a retired banker and had handled my accounts before Meg moved to town. He was a conservative, silk-turtleneck-and-cashmere-blazer kind of guy. I liked him.

Rhiza was Malcolm's second wife. Her maiden name was Golden and she was his secretary for about four months before his divorce was finalized. Some parishioners more unkind than I might call her a trophy wife. She was blonde, seemed just a tad ditsy and was definitely what I would consider "eye-candy"

63

although I would never voice such an opinion. His first wife, whom I also knew well, ended up with quite a settlement, a tennis pro named Rock Singleton and a condo in Myrtle Beach. Malcolm wasn't hurting either. About five years ago, he took some time to show me several banks in the Cayman Islands where I could keep a little mad money if I needed to. I'm pretty sure he had first hand experience with those bankers.

Malcolm steered me in the right direction when I had my Great Idea. Everyone has a Great Idea somewhere in the back of his brain. Mine just happened to pan out. My Great Idea was a device that hooked to your phone, much like a caller ID. What it did was to automatically track your long-distance, display your carrier, the cost of your call in cents per minute, the total cost of the current call, and a running total of your long distance phone bill on a per-month basis.

We worked out the mechanics, went through the legal process to require the long-distance carriers to release the billing information on demand, applied for a patent, built a prototype and were ready to go into production when I received a certified letter from one of the Baby Bells. They were willing to pay me close to two million dollars for the patent. Looking back, I might have made more by selling the device, but it never pays to be greedy. Malcolm said to take the cash—the phone companies would've tied it up in court so long that I never would've gotten it marketed. I suspect Malcolm made quite a chunk of change himself for giving me that advice. I had no problem with that and Malcolm and I are still good friends. Strangely enough, I have yet to see the device on the market but my stocks and investments did real well for a couple of years.

"Hi, Malcolm," I said, as the last strains of the *Credo* melted away. I turned off the truck and opened the door, stepping out into a glorious late October afternoon.

"Hayden," Malcolm greeted me.

"Hi, Rhiza," I said, being polite, but loving to hear her Marilyn

Monroe-type voice, a voice which defied all laws of physics by being both squeaky and husky at the same time—a voice which she had cultivated so long and so well that it would be a shame not to let her use it—especially on me.

"Hello, Hayden," she said, smiling, and dropping a quick wink on me from her upstage eye so Malcolm couldn't catch it.

I almost laughed, but managed to change it at the last second to a cross between a cough and a throat-clearing. Rhiza was quite a flirt, but Malcolm was in no danger from me. His net worth exceeded mine ten times over. Not that Rhiza was *only* interested in money.

Other members of the vestry were arriving. Billy Hixon, the Junior Warden, drove up in his white lawn maintenance truck. He owned and operated a pretty successful lawn service and the rest of the vestry figured that if they elected Billy Junior Warden, he'd mow the lawn and keep the grounds up at no charge. They were wrong. Oh, he did the job, all right—at his normal rate plus ten percent, which he gave back to the church as his tithe.

Carol Sterling, the granddaughter of the famous mayor, had been on the vestry off and on since I'd been at the church. Annette Passaglio, Katherine Barr, George Romanski, Logan Askew, my own Meg Farthing and about six others. It was a homogenous club. All white, all mid-to upper class. How many Episcopalians does it take to change a light bulb? Two. One to mix the martinis and the other to call the electrician.

We met in the parish hall. I started the meeting, since I hadn't given the agenda to anyone except Malcolm.

"As we all know," I began, "Willie was murdered in our church a week ago Friday night. It's my job, as the detective on the case, to ascertain the circumstances surrounding the crime and to try to discover who would have wanted to kill him."

I paused for effect. "The purpose of this meeting is for me to find out the substance of the sexual harassment charges that were filed against Willie."

All eyes turned at once to Mother Ryan as if expecting her to answer and the blood went from her neck straight to her gilded roots in about two seconds flat.

"This has nothing to do with why he was killed," she sputtered, her hands gripping the edge of the table.

"Why don't you let me decide," I said. "And anyway, I don't see how you could possibly know that." I let the last sentence slide out of my mouth in my most implicatory manner.

Malcolm rattled his papers conspicuously and spoke up immediately, looking down at his notes through the half-glasses sitting on the end of his nose.

"On October fourth, Loraine Ryan came before this vestry and filed a formal complaint against William Boyd for sexual harassment. She said he had made advances toward her, left crude and lascivious notes on her desk, asked her out repeatedly and attempted to kiss her on two occasions. She declined to produce these notes, stating that they had been destroyed. It was the consensus of the vestry that I meet with Willie and hear his version of the events.

"On October sixth, I had a meeting with Willie in which I asked him if these charges were true. He replied in the affirmative. I then informed him that if he continued this behavior, he would be terminated from this position. I made myself very clear and Willie indicated that there would be no more such trespasses.

"On October seventh, I sent a letter to each vestry member informing them of the action I had taken. I then received a phone call from Loraine demanding that I terminate...um...relieve Willie immediately of all further responsibility at St. Barnabas. I declined to do so.

"On October tenth, Willie was found dead in the choir loft. That's all I have. Anyone else?"

There wasn't a sound. Then Rhiza piped up.

"I think Willie was a fine man. It's just a shame what happened to him." She burst into tears and Malcolm put his arm around her.

I looked at Herself. "Loraine, do you have anything to say?" I asked.

"I do not," she hissed.

"Does anyone else have anything to add?"

No one did. But the collective finger was clearly pointing at the rector du jour.

Meg and I stopped by The Slab for dinner on the way home. I was always on the lookout for the perfect Reuben sandwich and I had finally talked William Peter Moss, the owner, into making one to my specifications.

Pete was twice divorced and not just coincidentally my old roommate from our sophomore year of college. In fact, Pete was one of the reasons I was in St. Germaine, a town I hadn't heard of until I met two people from this little berg while in college. Both of them were instrumental in getting me to take the job with the police force fifteen years ago. Pete was a good jazz saxophone player and had done a brief stint in the Army Band before taking his honorable discharge, returning to his home in St. Germaine and deciding, against all reason, to take over the family business.

Unfortunately for Pete, his given name, "William," had been abandoned in high school when his middle name was discovered by an unknown prankster and broadcast across the campus via the student grapevine. Having a moniker like "Pete Moss" didn't help his dating status, but eventually, like all humorous names— and I'm thinking here of a woman I happen to know in Asheville, Barb Dwyer—the people of St. Germaine became familiar with it and the joking became minimal. The new name stuck, and Pete Moss made his way to UNC where I, with just a few snickers, made his acquaintance.

Pete hadn't changed much since college. He had grown his ponytail back after his fling with Uncle Sam, although it was now graying and thinning on top, and he sported an occasional earring. He was partial to flowered Hawaiian shirts, jeans, sandals, and as far as I know, had not worn any underwear since we were roommates in 1975. This, at least, was his modus operandi in college, and I suspect that he remained true to his vision of a "truly free society" even throughout his army career. He used to favor recreational pharmaceuticals, but I'm sure that his indulgence is a thing of the past. I point that out to him often—as a friend *and* as a police officer.

"Pete. I need a Reuben," I called out as soon as I hit the door.

"Got it covered."

"Rye bread?" I said.

"Check," he replied.

I had gone over the litany of ingredients more times than I could remember.

"Three inches of corned beef. And not that store-bought pre-packaged corned beef that looks and tastes like reconstituted wallpaper either. Real corned beef, sliced to order."

"Check."

"Sauerkraut. Kosher."

"Check."

"Swiss cheese. Imported."

"Check."

"Thousand Island Dressing. Not Russian."

"Check."

Despite Pete's best efforts at obtaining the correct ingredients, I finally resorted to making a monthly trip to an Asheville deli, buying the perfect corned brisket, a round of Baby Swiss cheese, and three gallons of homemade sauerkraut and keeping them in his walk-in. Then I could order a Reuben whenever I felt the urge. This was one of those times. It was my comfort food. Meg ordered a vegi-kabob on rice and I got a cheap bottle of Chianti to finish off the sumptuous repast.

"What do you think?" she began, embracing the obvious topic of conversation.

"Well, I've been in this business a long time," I started philosophically.

"Knock it off. What do you think?"

"If she didn't do it, she's guilty of something. I don't know what exactly, but as soon as I find out, you'll be the first to know. That is, right after the bishop. May I have one of your onions?"

"She did it," Meg said. "I knew I didn't like her."

As we finished our meal, the door of The Slab swung open and the cowbell that hung on the inside of the door heralded the arrival of Malcolm and Rhiza.

"We just thought we'd stop in for a cup of coffee," squeaked Rhiza in her husky voice. "May we join you?"

"Sure," I said. "Pull up a chair."

Malcolm pulled a chair out for Rhiza and they sat down. Malcolm called to the waitress, "Two coffees, please."

Although Meg had never said anything, I had the feeling that she didn't really care for Rhiza in the way that most women don't care for wealthy men's beautiful and slender second wives. But I could be wrong. She did say to Malcolm, "So, what do you think?"

"I think Loraine is telling the truth," Malcolm said, as his coffee arrived at the table.

"Really," I said, more as a statement than a question. I had thought that Malcolm didn't really care for Mother Ryan. His defense of her was a bit of a surprise.

"I don't think she could have had anything to do with it," said Rhiza.

"So you say," I said, drinking the last of the Chianti. "I'm not inclined to be as charitable."

We chatted with the Walkers for about ten minutes, then excused ourselves. I drove Meg back to the church to pick up her car.

"Well, that was odd," I said as soon as the car pulled away from the curb.

"It's almost as though they came to find us to tell us Herself was innocent. How strange is that?"

"I don't know what to make of it. That's for sure," I said, shaking my head and pulling into the church parking lot. "Can you come on over?"

"I think so. Let me see what Mother's doing and then I'll be out. If I can't make it, I'll call you.

"Thanks," I said, giving her a kiss.

I sat watching her until she was in her car and pulling out of the lot. Then I pointed my truck for home.

Chapter 6

Standing there, sauerkraut and Swiss cheese dripping
down my chin and a shotgun pointed at my midsection by a
demented alto, my mind raced to find a reason for my immediate predicament. Perhaps it had started with Isabel. Yes,
that was it. It all became very clear.

I had met her last year when she came by my office. I
heard a knock at the door, looked up and quickly tried to
pick my eyeballs back up off the desk. Her lips quivered as
she stood in the doorway, her red hair drifting gently to
her shoulders. "I want to join the choir," she said in a
voice so low it belonged in a Popeye cartoon, a cartoon
starring Brutus, to whom she bore no resemblance other
than her voice. "I'm a soprano."

I wasn't taken in so easily. I'd been around the block a
few times. I've heard sopranos before and this wasn't one. I
reached slowly into my top drawer for my bachelor's degree.
Others? Yes I had others, but I wasn't ready to pull out
the heavy artillery yet and there was no use showing all
my virtues this early in the game.

"I know what you have in that drawer," she said
nonchalantly as she postured her way into a soprano-esque
pose. Her legs were long. So long they seemed to go clear
up to her ears. I wondered where she bought her dresses.
Legs-R-Us?

Yes, she had the moves all right, but the voice was
all wrong. I slid the drawer closed, catching my fingers
at the first knuckle, and muttered a curse from the Second
Book of Esdras.

I looked up to see if she was shocked. She hadn't moved.
Either she hadn't heard me or she was very familiar with
Apocryphal anathemas. And I had a feeling her hearing was
very good. I lit my cigar and pulled my hat down low over
my eyes.

I threw her a hymnal and she caught it on the first bounce.

"What's your favorite hymn?" I asked her through cigar-clenched teeth, puffs of smoke accentuating each syllable like the exhaust of a finely tuned automobile.

She threw the hymnal back to me without opening it.

"Es flog ein kleins Waldvögelein," she said, a dry smile playing on her lips.

Ah, the Woodbird. I knew the hymn. It was one of my favorites. A subtle tune, majestic in nature yet somehow humble, with just a hint of familiarity. I also knew it wasn't in this hymnal. She was toying with me, that much was obvious.

"What about 'How Great Thou Art?'" I asked slowly, trying to draw her into a trap of her own design.

"A Danish drinking song."

My eyes narrowed to the size of two small oysters. "O Sacred Head?"

"Bach chorales are not hymns. They don't belong in a hymnal."

Suddenly I knew who she was. It was obvious. Why hadn't I recognized her? She had graced the front cover of the Journal of Anglican Musicians Swimsuit Edition for four years running, although, to her credit, the pictorial essay didn't do her justice.

"Hello, Isabel."

"Hello, handsome. I was wondering when you'd recognize me."

Isabel Gerhardt. Great-great granddaughter of Paul Gerhardt, the German hymnodist, and wanted by the police in connection with the recent spectacular murder of the chairman of the Bishop's Commission on Church Music. She was also the foremost expert on 18th-Century German hymnody alive today. Her lectures were sold out until the murder.

scalpers got two hundred dollars a ticket.

"I didn't do it," she sobbed, turning on the tears as easily as some people turn on their radios. "You've got to believe me. I need your help."

They all need my help.

I got to church early on Sunday and headed to the office. The whole murder was still a puzzle, but I expected the lab report, which would be delivered tomorrow morning, to clear up quite a few things. This was the first murder to take place in St. Germaine since my administration and although I had a Criminal Justice degree and didn't skip all that many classes, I had been inventing our police procedure on the fly.

I took the first installment of *The Alto Wore Tweed* into the office and made enough copies for the choir. My usual modus operandi was to put a copy of what I termed "interesting reading" into each of the choir folders behind the first anthem.

I began the service with the Karg-Elert *Marche Triomphale* and the rest of the liturgy followed without incident until the sermon. It was at this point that Elaine Hixon, the Junior Warden's wife and one of the back row altos (a quasi-militant feminist group which we, in the choir, refer to as the BRAs) decided that the choir loft was just a bit warmer than she had thought it would be and began to take her sweater off. I have to presume that she wasn't wearing a blouse under her sweater because it was her objective to remove her garment while remaining vested in her black robe and white surplice. This is a Houdiniesque maneuver that women ostensibly do fairly regularly, but unfortunately for Elaine, while her arms were inside her robe, her bra somehow got caught on her sweater which was, at that point, already over her head. The ensuing struggle resembled a couple of woodchucks mugging a nun.

What was quite amusing for the choir also became very amusing for the congregation when an unnamed tenor, reading

The Alto Wore Tweed, let loose a guffaw just as Herself reached the pinnacle of her sermon. Most of the parishioners turned and looked up. It was at this point that Elaine's head popped through her choir robe. She saw the congregation looking up at her, tipped her chair sideways, and, with her arms totally immobile and no way to keep herself upright, fell onto the floor. Luckily she wasn't hurt, but the whole episode caused her and the rest of the alto section, to break into hysterical muffled laughter—the kind of laughter that, once started, probably couldn't be stopped unless I pulled out "Old Betsy" from underneath the organ bench. I admit I thought about it.

"Don't do it," said Meg, in a hushed whisper, seeing my eyes shift.

Other than this small flaw in the warp and woof of the tapestry of our devotion, the service finished up with no incidents. I put the final touches on the Bach *Meine Seele erhebt den Herren* fugue and Meg and I made our exit out the front doors, skipping coffee time and thereby avoiding, until tomorrow at least, the inevitable caustic comments from Herself. We were heading out for a quick picnic lunch before Darlene's funeral, scheduled for three o'clock at the Mountainview Cemetery.

We swung by The Slab, where they had our sandwiches waiting for us. I had taken advantage of the disrupted sermon to call in a quick to-go order on Meg's cell. Luckily she had The Slab on the auto dial.

"You have to set a better example for the choir," Meg said, as we stood at the counter and picked out a bottle of chilled chardonnay and some pasta to go with the chicken salad. "Calling in a lunch order during the sermon just will not do."

"Yes, you're right. I am suitably chastised," I said, paying for the lunch and ushering Meg out the door.

We had a nice spot picked out that we hadn't yet tried on our search for the perfect alfresco locale. Our culinary quest was hardly what you'd call "roughing it." In her trunk, Meg kept a folding table for two, a couple of chairs, a complete set of flatware and china, various condiments, a crystal vase that we placed on the table filled with whatever wildflowers were handy, cloth napkins, two wine glasses and a portable CD player.

"This is a great sandwich," said Meg between bites of the hard crusted bread surrounding a delicious chicken and chutney salad and eaten to the strains of a Haydn string quartet. "I'm glad you didn't shoot the altos."

"It never crossed my mind," I said laughing.

"It's almost a little too chilly for picnicking any more."

"I'm afraid so," I said. Shall we call it quits till next year?"

"Not yet. We may get one or two chances in November if we're lucky. If not, I'll put the picnicteria into winter storage and put my spare tire back into the trunk."

The wind was picking up and despite the sunshine, the temperature was beginning to drop as the cold front moved across the mountains.

As we finished our meal and were cleaning up, I suggested we swing by my place and pick up a couple of coats before the graveside service.

We arrived at the cemetery at about a quarter to three. The coffin was suspended over the hole in the ground and thanks to the recent good weather, the funeral home had dispensed with the tent that usually covered funeral parties. The temperature had already dropped into the low forties and the wind was beginning to pick up. We were glad to have our jackets.

Meg and I stood in the back and did a visual who's-who. The guest of honor had obviously arrived but the family wasn't here yet. I was sort of surprised to see Arlen Pearl. I didn't figure Arlen to be a sentimental kind of guy. There were a number of people from the Puckett's Sunday school class at St. Germaine Baptist Church and a few from The Antique Barn, where Darlene worked. Maybell Lewis was in attendance. She was a member of Darlene's ecumenical prayer group and attended Friendship Baptist Temple, a Black congregation in Boone. I had talked to her on a number of occasions while shopping for antiques.

The limousine pulled up at five minutes before three. The funeral home in charge of the burial was Swallow's Mortuary, one of several that operated in Boone and made routine visits to the Mountainview Cemetery. Carlton Puckett and some folks who I suspected were Darlene's family got out first. Brother Ralph Simpson from St. Germaine Baptist and a couple of funeral suits, who I recognized but didn't know by name, followed closely and made their way to the seats. Brother Ralph assumed the helm.

"Dearly beloved, we are gathered here today..."

Meg elbowed me. "I think he's doing a wedding," she whispered.

"Shhh."

"...to bid farewell to our sister Darlene."

"Whew," whispered Meg out of the side of her mouth. "That was close."

"But as sad as we are to lose Darlene we know that she leaped out of that sunroof and STRAIGHT INTO THE ARMS OF JESUS!" shouted Brother Ralph. "Halleluia!"

"Yooooowwwww," howled Maybell, putting a handkerchief over her face.

"She is now walking the streets of gold. There are no potholes in those streets. There is no hunger on those streets. And do you know why?" Brother Ralph asked, getting into a rhythm.

I don't know if he was expecting a response, but Maybell was from a denomination that answered questions that were asked from the pulpit.

"'Cause, those are the STREETS OF GLORY!" Maybell shrieked as she fell into a half swoon.

Brother Ralph, not used to such interaction, now had an audible congregation of one, and he wasn't about to let this opportunity pass. The sermon went on for a good thirty minutes, touching on the apocalypse, the last judgment, the rapture, the four-step plan of salvation, the parable of the mustard seed, and Noah's Ark. I was pretty sure it wasn't a scripted sermon, but it was heartfelt and Maybell lent her vocal stylings as punctuation to the high points.

"Yes! Yes! Tell it all, brother!"

Brother Ralph was preaching up to a grand finale when the funeral director noticed something amiss. He was standing off to the left of the makeshift pulpit, facing the mourners and nodding his head at appropriate moments when suddenly his focus changed. His eyes narrowed and he squinted up into the sun which, at this time of year, was fairly low in the sky and directly behind us. His mouth dropped open and he pulled a pair of sunglasses out of his inside suit pocket and put them on, his eyes never leaving the spot above our heads.

Brother Ralph stopped his sermon in mid-invitation for the first time in his preaching career—a career which he began at age twelve as a child evangelist and which he assumed would continue until the day he died. "I'll quit telling people about Jesus when I've drawn my last breath," he would say. I believed him.

He stopped preaching because he was having a vision. Directly behind us, about thirty feet in the air and coming out of the sun right toward Brother Ralph, was a woman. A naked woman, her form surrounded and illuminated by the sun's deepening rays. This was the vision that stopped him in midsentence. We all turned and looked up.

After three days of drifting on the autumn thermals, one of the missing dolls was coming down quickly thanks to the wind which had picked up and, I suspected, the drastic change in temperature.

"Hey, she's one of mine," Arlen said to Meg under his breath.

"Really," said Meg, hissing back. "Can you prove it? I'm sure there are lots of helium-filled sex toys floating around the mountain."

"No, she's mine all right. I got the receipt."

Meg rolled her eyes.

The doll floated directly above our heads. Arlen leaped up into the air, grabbed the doll by its foot, pulled her down and tucked her under one arm.

Brother Ralph was at a loss for words for perhaps the first time in his life. He couldn't quite remember what he was talking about.

"Um...and so therefore sisters and brothers...let us praise the Lord. Amen."

"Amen. Halleluia!" sang out Maybell.

"He wrapped it up nicely," I noted.

That evening I received a call from Nancy. Meg was at her house and I took the opportunity to enjoy a Cuban—a *Romeo y Julietta*—my cigar of choice, illegal in this country due to the embargo, but smuggled in for me by a member of the St. Barnabas Youth Group coming home from a mission trip in Costa Rica.

"I heard about the funeral."

"It was something," I said, puffing away and trying to be as circumspect as possible.

"Anyway," she said, "I was just on the phone with Kent Murphee in Boone."

Kent was the coroner.

"And he wants to meet with you tomorrow at 8:30."

"8:30? What for?"

"Something about the lab report on Willie Boyd."

"Jeez," I whined. "8:30?"

Nancy laughed. "8:30 *in the morning*. 'Night, boss."

The next morning found me in Kent's office at 8:32. It was early for me, but I was nothing if not a dedicated professional.

"Good morning, Hayden. How 'bout a drink?" asked Kent as I walked in.

"It's 8:30 in the morning," I said. "And I'm a dedicated professional. What have you got?"

"Bourbon okay?"

"Fine with me. Just one though."

Kent poured a couple of fingers of Maker's Mark into two of his old fashioned specimen glasses that I knew he kept on hand for just such occasions. Kent was always in a vest and a tweed jacket, summer or winter, and sucking on a pipe which, most of the time, remained unlit.

"Give me the good news," I said, sipping my breakfast cocktail.

"Interesting stuff," Kent said, pulling out a file and opening it on his desk. "The food you sent over was clean—although some of it was quite old. The wine in the bottle was negative for poison. It was just wine. And not very good wine either. I'd say about six dollars a bottle."

"They can tell that with an analysis?" I asked.

"Yep. Plus I saw the price on the bottom of the bottle."

"Very funny," I chuckled. "What else?"

"The wine in Mr. Boyd's stomach was negative for poison also. In fact, he had no poison in his stomach at all."

"So how did he die?"

"Poison."

"Brought on by poison, I suppose," I said, laughing. "You know," I said, taking another sip, "whenever I walk in here, I feel like I've fallen into an Abbott and Costello routine."

It was Kent's turn to chuckle. "In point of fact, he died of a heart attack. But it was the poison that caused his heart to stop. The report on the stomach contents shows no poison present, but his blood contained cardiac glycosides—specifically oleandrin, nerin, digitoxigenin, and olinerin of which oleandrin is the principal toxin. Also present was rosagenin, which has definite strychnine effects."

"In English please, Kent," I begged.

"In English," said Kent, "Mr. Boyd was killed by one of the oldest techniques for ending an unhappy marriage known in these hills. Oleander poisoning. I would say yellow oleander, the leaves as well as the bark which would be indicated by the presence of the rosagenin. Nasty and potent stuff."

"What do you mean 'for ending an unhappy marriage'?" I asked.

"Well, before divorce became the legal institution it is today, it was very difficult for a woman to rid herself of an unfaithful or abusive husband. Generally a cup of oleander tea would take care of the problem. The heart attack that resulted was very rarely diagnosed as poison. Although the deceased would generally vomit and there would be an agonized expression on the corpse's face...."

"Like Willie."

"Exactly. But usually the expression could be relaxed and the body would be cleaned and dressed by the family before the undertaker ever arrived. Here's the interesting thing. When a woman could file for no-fault divorce herself, the mortality rate of married males ages twenty to fifty went down sixty percent."

"You're kidding," I said.

"I'm not," Kent replied. "There wasn't any poison in the stomach so we checked his mouth. Sure enough, the membranes inside were covered with the stuff. And the oral membranes can absorb substances very quickly."

"But he didn't swallow it?"

"Nope."

"This is curiouser and curiouser," I said, quoting Mr. Dodgson.

On my way home I got a page from Marilyn Forbis, the church secretary.

"I don't know if this means anything," she said when I called her back, "but Willie came in to get some keys on the Friday morning before he was killed."

"He did?"

"I remember the time, because he came into the office while I was typing the bulletin. I had to get it finished, so I gave him the whole ring. He said he'd lost his."

"Did he bring them back?"

"After about an hour."

"Were they all there?"

"Yeah. I checked. They're all here." She paused. "Sorry, Hayden. I forgot all about it till last night. Does it mean anything?"

"I don't know," I said. "Maybe."

Chapter 7

Denver was content to let me figure out the puzzle as she settled into a Naugahyde chair across from my desk. My mind traveled back to the year before—or maybe the year before that.

The air was cold—cold as the shoulder Isabel gave me when I invited her out to share a cigar. As I walked down the deserted street, pulling my hat down over my eyes and heading for my favorite fern-bar, I mentally reviewed the case as Isabel laid it out.

It was a new priest causing all the trouble. One thing about this guy—he wasn't afraid to fire people and that included choir members. In his church, if you didn't sing professionally, you didn't sing. It wasn't my cup of tea, but I've had paid choirs before and there's something to be said for singing the Byrd "Sacerdotes Domini" with one six-minute rehearsal right before the service.

So when he took charge, his first order of business was to replace the choir. Oh, they were given a chance all right. A chance to sight-read from the 1524 "Geystliche gesang Buchleyn." This whole setup smelled like last week's halibut.

I walked across the street and into an alley beside the bar, the wind whipping across my shoulders like the flagellation of some unseen monk. It was cold and turning colder. What was I doing? I didn't have time for this. I had hymns to pick. Then I remembered the money. Two hundred a day would buy a lot of stogies. I lit one up in anticipation.

"You know," Meg commented, lounging in front of a roaring fire and reading my masterpiece over a glass of Black Opal Merlot, "your story doesn't really have a plot. I mean you have five installments and absolutely nothing has happened."

"I was hoping no one would notice. I'm a writer. I can't be concerned with a plot. And I think you'll find that after one more glass of wine, the plot won't matter nearly as much."

"In that case, pour."

After getting the report on Willie's demise, we decided to go ahead and bury him on the following Wednesday—almost two weeks after he'd been killed. He had a nice service in the church— although not very well attended—and then a burial that St. Barnabas paid for. We couldn't find any next of kin. Mother Ryan had declined to perform the burial rites so I had called Father Tim from a couple of parishes away and he was happy to oblige. Meg and I kept scouring the skies for another airborne visitor but our efforts were unrewarded.

Our choir rehearsal that evening went very well. The choir was rehearsing the *Missa Brevis St. Johannis de Deo* for All Saints Sunday, just two weeks away. It was a lovely little Haydn mass and one of the choir's favorites. We rehearsed in the choir room as we always did and then went up to the loft to go over it once with the organ and the two violinists who had come up from Appalachian State to accompany us.

I was the last into the choir loft, having stopped in the choir room for the pertinent scores and parts for the violinists. Nancy met me at the top of the stairs.

"Hi there, Nancy. Can I talk you into joining the choir?"

"I don't think so. I have a lousy voice. I did enjoy my one class in music appreciation though."

"Yeah? How did you do?" I asked. I myself had taught music appreciation on several occasions.

"I made a C," she confessed. "I had an A going into the final but on the exam I said that 'parallel organum' was a method of musical gratification frowned on by early church fathers. I won't even tell you my definition of a faggott. I thought it was pretty funny, but the prof was not amused. He was sort of an early music freak."

"Yep, you do have to be careful," I said, making my way over to the organ, Nancy following closely. "They do not suffer nonbelievers gladly." The rest of the choir was still trying to find their seats.

"Anyway," Nancy said leaning over the console and lowering her voice, "we found the rest of the wine."

"Really? Let me guess. Willie Boyd's house."

"Nope. In the trunk of his car. Dave and I thought we'd wait for you before we searched his house. How'd you know he had it?"

I handed the violin parts over to the players.

"I didn't really. Just a hunch. Who else would have taken it? Bud? He didn't want it. He really has better taste in wine. Then I remembered the lock on the closet that Willie supposedly 'fixed.' It was the same old rusted mechanism. There was never anything wrong with it. Remember? The key stuck in the lock just like it always did. So when Willie called in to the station, he was just covering his tracks."

"Well, aren't you something?" said Nancy in what I took to be an admiring tone.

"Stick with me kid. That's why I get paid the big bucks. You want to hang around and listen to this?" I asked pointing to the violinists. "You'll like it."

"Well, my social calendar is rather full, this being a Wednesday evening and all. But thank you. I believe I will."

As I sat down and fired up the Beast—the choir's term of endearment for the organ—I saw, perched conspicuously on the music rack, a piece of paper neatly folded in half. A note from Herself, I figured, as I picked it up and unfolded it.

I saw who did it. It's Him. It's Matthew.
O hark the herald angels sing;
The boy's descent which lifted up the world.

84

I put it back on the rack as carefully as I could, covered it with a book of chorale preludes and called Nancy over to the console.

"Don't leave until rehearsal is over. We need to talk." She nodded.

The problem with reading something like that note right before you are called on to play the Haydn *Little Organ Mass* and direct the choir and the violins all at the same time, is that it makes it incredibly difficult to concentrate on the task at hand. I knew that I wasn't at my best, but when Marjorie put her flask back into her hymnal rack, reached over, patted me on the arm and said, "What's wrong Hayden? You're playing like a pig," I realized my mind wasn't multitasking like I thought it was. I snapped back to the job at hand and finished the rehearsal with a flash of majestic flourishes worthy of any police detective. The choir was vocally appreciative.

I thanked the cheering throng and the somewhat stunned violinists for their efforts and sent them home beseeching them to practice hard, knowing in my heart that they wouldn't look at the music again until Sunday. Still, it was my job to entreat them just as it was their job to ignore my counsel. It was a delicate balance of natural laws that could not be disrupted for fear of reprisals on a cosmic scale. As the choir made their way back to the choir room downstairs to put their music away, Nancy sidled up to the organ.

"What's up?"

I picked the note up by the edges and laid it gently on a music stand which I had tipped to the horizontal position. "I doubt if there are any prints, but let's send it to the lab anyway."

Nancy read the note. "What is this? A confession? A clue? A joke?"

"It would be hard to say just yet."

"Who is Matthew? Do you know him?"

I thought for a moment. "No Matthews in the choir. There's a Matthew Aaron in the congregation. He's a real estate attorney.

Matthew Siegenthaler works in a nursery. Those are the only two I know in town."

"What about last names?" Nancy asked.

"I'll get Dave to check them."

I saw who did it. It's Him. It's Matthew.

"If someone saw who did it, why leave a note? Why not just tell us?" Nancy asked, thinking out loud. I'm afraid she was picking up quite a few of my bad habits. I wondered if she had started smoking cigars. It was only a matter of time.

"Well now, that's the question, isn't it?" I pulled my list out of my pocket and smoothed it out on the top of the organ.

"What's that?" said Nancy with a derisive snort.

"It's my check-list."

"You're kidding, of course. No one has a check-list."

I ignored her rude comments and went through the litany for her benefit as well as my own.

When?

Willie Boyd was still killed on Friday afternoon. 5:12 p.m.—give or take. JJ was the last to see him, other than the witness—if is there was one—and maybe the killer. He pilfered the wine earlier that afternoon and drank from one of the bottles. It wasn't poisoned, however.

Who?

Don't know. But apparently we have a witness and a clue (if that's what it is). Who is Matthew?

Why?

I still didn't know of any enemies that Willie might have had. Mother Ryan was acting very suspicious about the sexual harassment charge. I suspected that most of the charges were trumped up, but why? And why did Willie admit to them? Maybe he had some dirt on the priestess and she wanted him gone. Fired maybe, but killed? I doubted it. Still, I had the feeling that Loraine Ryan was the key.

How?

This we knew. Oleander poisoning. But it wasn't found in Willie's stomach. The poison entered his system through his mouth, absorbed though the membranes, but was not swallowed.

What?

What? Still a stupid question.

The next morning Nancy, Dave and I sat in The Slab over a pot of coffee and a plate of assorted doughnuts and looked at a photocopy of the note. We sent the original to the lab to scan it for prints but I wasn't hopeful.

"OK, Dave, did you check the phone listings?"

Dave checked his notes. "Yeah, boss. I used our CD-ROM directory. There are three Matthews in town. The two you mentioned plus Matthew Blake, a retired building contractor from Tampa. There are nine others further out in the county. Two last-name Matthews. One Mathews with one 't.' I'll check on them all this afternoon."

"It's probably not them, but check anyway," I said and picked up the note, holding it up to look at it. "It was a laser printer I think. A common font. Maybe New York or something in that family."

Nancy nodded. "But what about the second two lines?"

O hark the herald angels sing;
The boy's descent which lifted up the world.

"It's a hymn, isn't it?"

"Sort of. The first line is almost 'Hark the herald angels sing,' but not quite."

"Is it in our hymnal?" Nancy asked.

"Yeah, in the Christmas section."

"I still don't understand," said Dave, breaking in, "why someone would leave you some sort of cryptic note. Why not just tell you? And why all the mystery?"

I put the note back on the table and picked up a cruller, dunking it into my coffee before downing half the pastry in one majestic munch. I did however take time to swallow. I'm not a total Neanderthal.

"Well, we have a couple of choices. It could be that the murderer thinks he's so much smarter than us that he wants to test our intellects by leaving obtuse clues."

Dave was staying with me, doughnut for doughnut. "You think that's it?"

"Nope. I think someone saw the murder or at least knows who did it. They can't or don't want to tell us directly. I don't know why yet."

Nancy interrupted, "So you think it's actually a clue to the murderer?"

"I do. Mostly because it's all we have right now. And someone had to know about the killing besides the murderer. It's very rare that there's only one person who's involved. Yep," I said, polishing off the other half of the cruller and washing it down with a gulp of coffee, "it's a puzzle all right."

That afternoon, Dave and I went over to Willie Boyd's apartment. The landlord was waiting at the door for us.

"Can I move his stuff outta there?"

"Let us look around. We'll let you know."

Willie's apartment consisted of one sixteen-by-sixteen room and a small bathroom. His furniture included a single bed, pushed against the wall, a kitchen table of sorts with one chair, and an old television set with rabbit ears sitting on a couple of concrete blocks. There was a beat-up microwave on the table and an old fabric-covered extension cord that had to be close to forty years old connecting it to an outlet. The kitchen, what there was of it, consisted of a sink and a small refrigerator, vintage early 60's. The bed had no sheets or blankets, but rather was covered with an old sleeping bag that had been unzipped, opened up and spread across the mattress. The one pillow had no case and was covered in grease stains, presumably from Willie's unwashed hair. There was a stack of newspapers piled to the side of the bed, the most recent from August—almost three months ago. Almost all of them were unread judging from their unopened condition.

"Doesn't look like there's anything here, boss," said Dave. "Hardly any clothes, no personal effects."

"Hmmm." I was looking toward the counter in the kitchenette where there were two bottles of unopened wine. I went over, picked them up and looked at the labels. *Quinta do Crasto* and *Quinta do Valle do Dora Maria*, both 1999 vintages from Portugal.

"Now where do you suppose Willie would have gotten these?" I muttered to no one in particular.

Dave scratched his head.

"Well there haven't been any reports of any wine thefts lately. Maybe he bought them."

"I don't think so. I'll bet we find that these go for about twenty bucks a bottle. That's more than Willie would spend on two week's worth of hooch."

We checked the rest of Willie's room and, finding nothing we considered case-breaking, gave the landlord permission to clean it out. Of course, the wine went with us.

Chapter 8

Dear Choir:

I think that it is time that we approach with reverent awe that celebration which makes us truly Protestant (not Baptist though, because the Baptists claim they are direct descendants of John THE Baptist and I'm not about to dispute them.) I'm speaking of Reformation Day—the day on which, in 1517, Martin Luther set us free from the control of the Roman Church by nailing his ninety-five theses to the door of the church at Wittenberg proclaiming his dissatisfaction with certain papal decrees. It is fitting and proper therefore, that we should celebrate the foremost contribution by Martin Luther to the Protestant cause. No, not throwing the yoke of Catholic oppression off our shoulders, but something far, far more consequential.

As we head full-steam into the holiday season, we need only to turn to our history books to find that Martin Luther offers us a surefire way to lose 15 pounds before Thanksgiving. Yes, I'm talking about the DIET OF WURMS.

By now you are saying to yourselves, "Well, I've heard of the Diet of Wurms, of course. Every scholar of comparative religion has—but does it really work?" I can assure you it does. I saw actual testimonials on Ricki Lake. By all accounts, Brother Martin lost about fifteen pounds from November 1 to November 8, 1521 and we have just obtained from an unnamed monk in upstate New York the actual manuscript of this famous diet. So now, after 474 years, we present to you—straight from the Reformation—

Martin Luther's DIET OF WURMS
The only Diet of Wurms with the International Congress of Church Musicians (ICCM) Seal of Approval

Day One

Breakfast	Two Wurms over easy
Lunch	One slice of Wurmy bread, Wurm salad
Dinner	Earthwurm enchilada

Day Two

Breakfast	Wurm omelet
Lunch	One-half bagel with wurm spread
Dinner	Cream of Wurm soup

Day Three

Breakfast	Wurms Benedict, 2 Wurm halves on lettuce
Lunch	Wurmloaf (w/sauce)
Dinner	Centipede Pie and Gummy Wurms

Day Four

Breakfast	Hash Brown Wurms, Wurm Biscuit (1), Cream of Wurm Cereal (one bowl)
Lunch	Wurm Pasta (3 cups uncooked)
Dinner	Flatwurm Flambé

Day Five

Breakfast	*Wurmy apples (1)*
Lunch	*6 wurms heated on the sidewalk*
Dinner	*Any wurms found under the doormat*

Day Six

Breakfast	*Chipped roundwurm on toast*
Lunch	*Slug Chowder*
	(2 crackers with weevils)
Dinner	*Ringwurm Crêpes*

Day Seven

Breakfast	*Night Crawler Yogurt (1 cup)*
Lunch	*A Wurm Pita w/ mustard*
Dinner	*Mock Leg of Wurm*

So there you have it. A sure fire way to lose 15 lbs. before Thanksgiving. If you care to read more about the Diet of Wurms check out a book in your local library. (I'm sure they have all the nutritional information available.)

Grace and Peace,
Hayden

"My darling, I fear your current offering may be a bit too theologically obscure for the average chorister. How many, do you suppose, have even heard of the Diet of Wurms?" Meg asked, rather too sarcastically, I thought.

"I cannot and I will not recant anything. Here I stand. I can do no other."

"Yes, Dr. Luther, Very funny. Are you running out of steam on *The Alto Wore Tweed?"* Megan wondered aloud as she finished reading my latest missive. "At least we understood *some* of that."

"I just thought that Reformation Day needed a little punching up. It's not one of our more well-known feast days. I'll get back to the story in a bit."

"So what do we actually do for Reformation Day? I don't seem to remember any kind of mention of it in the service."

"Well, usually we all dress up as monks, walk barefoot in procession down Main Street and nail our complaints to the mayor's door. Then we find a hotdog vendor and say 'Make us one with everything.' But we haven't done it for a few years. Actually the last time was right before you moved here."

She nodded thoughtfully. "This is a tradition I think we should resurrect. Do you still have your monk suit?"

"Of course I have my monk suit. Is it always your habit to be so inquisitive?" I added, smirking poignantly. I had a lot of monk jokes.

"Oh, haha," Meg replied mirthlessly. "Your puns garner you no lady's favors, sirrah. And what's this stuff about the International Congress of Church Musicians? I haven't ever heard of them."

"It's a secret society and I must advise you to pretend you never asked that question."

Meg looked up at me from below arched eyebrows.

"Many people have made that same inquiry in various forms and were never heard from again."

"Do tell," she said.

"Sometimes they'd ask nicely and say, 'Just what is the purpose and mission of the ICCM?' and sometimes they'd just yell, 'It's three o'clock in the morning! Why don't you idiots shut up and get that damn goat off my lawn?' Then the cops would come and we'd have a heck of a time explaining sixteen men in raccoon hats, a goat and a five-gallon container of spaghetti sauce."

"I see. So *that's* what you're up to all hours of the night."

"I have no comment at this time."

"You need to have your blood sugar checked. I think you may be a couple of bubbles out of plumb. Now, let's see that clue you were talking about."

I pulled a Xerox of the clue out of my shirt pocket, unfolded it, put it on the kitchen table and smoothed it out. Meg spun it around slowly so she could read it and sat down at the table.

"Hmmm," she hummed, deep in thought.

"Any ideas?" I rested my elbows on the table and propped my chin in my hands.

"OK," she said. "Let's assume for the moment that this is a real clue. That someone saw who did it and is trying to get you to guess who it is—for whatever reason."

"Fair enough."

I saw who did it. It's Him. It's Matthew.

She continued. "It's obviously not Matthew, right?"

I nodded. "All Matthews are currently alibied."

"Then what could 'Matthew' mean? Her fingers were tapping on the table.

"The Gospel of Matthew?" I offered.

"Right," she said decisively. "But where in the gospel? That's the question."

I was content to let her keep going. I had a feeling Meg was going to make me look good.

"Hmmm," she hummed again, this time at a slightly higher pitch.

"Got it!" she sang out suddenly. "Get me a hymnal and a Bible!"

"An Episcopal hymnal?"

"Of course, silly. It's so obvious. It has to be an Episcopal hymnal and whatever translation of the Bible we use at the church. You're so cute when you're playing detective," she called after me as I went into the library to fetch her books.

I handed her a New American Standard version of the Bible and The Hymnal 1982.

"Now," she said picking up the hymnal and turning to the index in the back. "*Hark, the Herald Angels*, hymn number 87. You see? It's Him, It's Matthew. *O hark the herald angels sing.* Hymn number 87. Matthew 8:7. Pretty clever, yes?"

"You're a wonder, do you know that?" I said admiringly. "How about a kiss?"

"Not now! Can't you see we're about to solve the murder? All we have to do is look up the verse and we'll know who the killer is." She was already thumbing through the well worn book.

"And he said to him 'I will come and heal him,'" I quoted.

"What?" she said, distracted and finding the passage."

"And he said to him 'I will come and heal him,'" I repeated. "Matthew 8:7."

"How did you know that? Do you have this whole book memorized?" She was genuinely shocked.

"Well, no. Actually I looked it up this morning."

"You stinker!" she shouted, laughing. "I might have known."

"Now, about that kiss, Ms. Farthing...."

"Not on your life. Get away from me. Lips that touched goat lips will never touch mine." She ducked under my halfhearted grope and slid to the other side of the table.

"Well then, who did it?" she asked, picking up the note again and looking at it intently as if the answer would leap forth from the paper. "A doctor?"

"It could be, but that's still a stretch. It's certainly not a definite identification of the killer. There have to be eight or ten doctors in the church not to mention dentists, nurses, EMTs, and whoever else might be employed in the health care field. And let's not forget, it may be someone that isn't a member."

"I think it is," said Meg suddenly quiet, her playful mood dropping away. "I think it is a member of St. Barnabas."

October was drawing to a close. It was my favorite month and this one was certainly one for the books. The mayor had called me in to see about our progress on the case. Of course, the mayor was also known as Pete Moss, the owner of The Slab.

"How're you doing Hayden?"

"Is this an *Official Meeting*?" I asked. "'Cause if it is, I want a complimentary piece of Boston Cream pie and a cup of coffee."

"Yes, it's official. Doris," he called, "get the detective some pie and a cup of coffee, would you?"

"Boston Cream," I yelled out.

Pete dragged up a chair. "The city council wants to know about your progress on the Boyd case."

"Ah, the council."

"Any progress?"

"Some," I said. "Not very much though."

The pie and coffee arrived right on schedule. I always enjoyed these high-level meetings.

"That's it?" asked Pete.

"That's it."

Pete nodded and his eyebrows went up. "Well, thanks for coming in."

"Always a pleasure," I muttered, my mouth full of the scrumptious pastry.

I pulled up to the McCollough's trailer later that afternoon. Moosey met me at the door, grinning, with his hands behind him and rocking back and forth on his heels. This time I hadn't forgotten.

"Here you go, young man," I said, handing him a big bag of M&Ms. He was out the door and down the steps in half a second.

"Moosey," his mother called after him. Don't eat those before dinner." She sighed and turned to me with a mock frown showing on her face.

"You shouldn't oughtta give him that stuff."

"OK, I'll try to cut back."

"Well, thanks," she said. "C'mon in. Is this about Bud?"

"No, actually it's not. I came to get some expertise and maybe a little advice."

"Sure," she said, confused. "Have a seat." She motioned to the couch and took a chair facing it.

"Do you know anything about oleander?" I asked.

The color drained out of Ardine McCollough's face so fast I thought she was going to pass out. If I had had a polygraph on her, it would have been playing Chopsticks.

"Um...it's a plant, I think," she stuttered, her voice in a half-whisper, her hand moving to her collar.

Whatever skills Ardine might possess, I could tell that lying was not going to be one of them. I hadn't even posed a pointed question and already she was ready to confess. I admit that I now had an idea what had happened to PeeDee McCollough, but that wasn't why I was here.

"Listen, Ardine," I said. "I'm not here to cause you any trouble. I figure PeeDee just up and left. It happens a lot around here and I'm sure that you're glad he's gone."

"I am glad," she replied, relaxing just a little but still sitting stiffly in the chair, her hands clenched and primly in her lap.

"But there was someone else in town killed by oleander," I continued, "and I want to know if anyone called you for some advice."

"I don't know if I should say," said Ardine, her voice quiet and without emotion. "I promised I wouldn't."

"And I know your promise is important," I said, leaning forward to impart the importance of the question. "But I need to know who it is."

"Yes. I guess you should know."

I waited for about six beats, not saying anything.

"It was that woman from the church."

"The priest?"

"No. The one that works in the kitchen. She said her name was JJ."

For someone who has a comment for every occasion, I was speechless.

Chapter 9

The smoke of my stogie circled my head as I rounded the corner of the bar. Then I saw her. She caught my eye like that little fish hook that your brother casts over his shoulder without paying attention. A long, tall blonde. I'd seen her before--the bishop's personal trainer.

"Hi handsome," she purred. "I'm Amber. Amber Dawn."

"Hi Amber. I saw your photo spread last month in 'Hymns and Hers.' Very impressive."

"Thanks babe. I've been looking for you. The bishop wants you to take a look at this."

She handed me a memo. It was from the bishop all right and I was his church music commission toady. I opened the memo and gave it the once over. Another PCD--Politically Correct Directive.

"Beginning immediately," the memo said, "all new music compositions must contain a minimum of 50% 'nonwhite' notes. (Also, in keeping within the national and diocesan guidelines, all whole and half notes will be known as 'pigmentally impoverished.')

"As church musicians, we must also be aware that, although albino-genetic recessive notes tend to move faster and jump higher than pigmentally impoverished notes, we must not perpetuate this stereotype. Pigmentally impoverished notes must be allowed to achieve their true and full potential, and not be held back by any of the 'so called' traditional composers. By the same token, notes-of-color must be allowed to proceed at their own pace."

I had heard it all before, but now the bishop was taking it up a notch.

Christmas, as always, was coming up too fast. I planned to enjoy the holidays every year, but it never worked out. My Christmas vacation generally started on December 26th.

In addition to my church duties, which multiplied during the holidays, there was a myriad of constabulary duties that needed taking care of, not the least of which was this murder. Now more than six weeks old, it was out of the thoughts of almost everyone else. However, I am nothing if not dogged, and I was pretty sure I would have it wrapped up by Christmas.

After speaking with Ardine McCollough, my next visit in the case of the dearly departed Willie Boyd was to JJ. I found her, after a couple of misses, in the kitchen back at the church fixing something for the evening fellowship meal.

"Hi there, Hayden. Wassup?" JJ was dumping a pile of what I hoped were vegetables recognized by the USDA into the boiling pot.

"Well, not too much, my dear. What's cooking today?"

JJ was sporting her ever-present white painter's overalls with one of the straps dangling down over her shoulder, a flannel shirt, a bandanna around her neck, and a baseball cap.

"I can't decide what kind of soup it's going to be. I'm just putting the stock together."

"Smells good."

"You can have some tonight if you get here on time for a change."

"I'll do my best."

I poured a cup of coffee and leaned against the counter. I tried to act nonchalant, but couldn't pull it off.

"I've got to ask you something, JJ."

"Well, go on then," she said, stirring the pot with her canoe paddle.

I took a sip, then said, "What do you know about oleander?"

"Oh, hell!" she said, stopping for a moment and looking at

me, then turning her attention back to the soup. "I knew some-one would find out sooner or later."

I was shocked. Almost as shocked as when Ardine gave me JJ's name in the first place.

"JJ, I've got to tell you, I think you should get a lawyer."

"Why? Is that crazy woman going to press charges?"

"It's out of her hands," I said, thinking that Herself probably wouldn't hesitate in letting JJ walk. There was no love lost between Willie and Mother Ryan. "It's our jurisdiction, but an indictment will have to be brought."

"An indictment? What are you talking about?"

"I'm talking about oleander poisoning." I said, as seriously as I could.

"Yeah, well. I guess I'm guilty then." JJ said. "But I've got to tell you, I was just sick and tired of it."

"I understand," I said, nodding and not understanding at all. "What was the final straw? The wine?"

"The wine? There wasn't any wine. I just thought it was time I did something."

"So you used the oleander?"

"Well," she said, "It's virtually untraceable. And it's only dangerous to the thing that consumes it. If we ate the meat afterwards, there wouldn't be any risk and no one would ever know," she said matter-of-factly, as she continued to stir the soup.

"If we...ate the meat...*afterwards,*" I said, slowly, trying desperately to make sense of this conversation.

"Yep," she said, reaching down beside the counter and pick-ing up a wrinkled brown grocery bag with the top rolled down. She handed it to me. It weighed close to twenty pounds. "I wasn't going to tell anyone."

I opened the bag and looked in.

"Hedgehogs?" I asked, not really believing what I was seeing. "You were poisoning Mrs. McCarty's hedgehogs?" JJ lived next door to the eccentric pet breeder.

"They're all in my yard and they're crawling in my heating ducts. There was one stuck in my dryer last week. It crawled up through the vent and lodged itself in the heating unit. It cost me a hundred-and-twenty bucks to get the dryer fixed, and my clothes all smelled like roast duck. That's when I came up with the idea."

"What idea?"

"Roasted hedgehog soup."

"Ahhh. Come to think of it, I don't think I'll be here for dinner this evening."

"Well, don't tell anyone. Almost no one knows and I don't want to spoil the surprise."

"Almost no one?" I asked.

"Yeah, last week when I was mixing up the oleander, Mother Ryan was in here getting some coffee. I might have told her I had some pests I needed to get rid of. She might figure it out."

"I doubt it," I said smiling. "She's got bigger problems."

The boy's descent which lifted up the world.
It bothered me, that last line.

Mother Ryan was getting ready for her fifteen minutes of fame. She had finagled the bishop into allowing her to host a conference for women priests. Of course, on the brochures it said *wimmyn* priests and she had contacted all the appropriate news groups to make sure the conference was well-covered, at least in ecumenical circles. She discovered when she spelled womyn with a "y," the reporters came running.

The first week of Advent was when her conference was to take place. *ReImagining God the Mother in the Twenty-First Century* was the cognomen the wimmyn had chosen to celebrate their collective ecufem consciousness. Three days of speeches, seminars and services. Along with the three leaders, there were twenty-three women priests signed up and at least that many reporters booked into the B&Bs. The priests were staying with parishioners. The reporters were on expense accounts. And although I was ordered by Herself to be present to play for the services, I was planning on staying as far away as possible.

I knocked on Mother Ryan's office door and waited for the requisite "Come!" uttered as a command rather than a polite request. I think she heard the fractured greeting in a police drama on television and decided it demonstrated her authority. Hearing the dictate, I opened the door and entered her rather masculine study, which she had appointed herself and charged to the decorating committee's budget, much to their consternation. Leather and walnut—a nice combination.

"Yes?" she asked curtly as she looked up from the papers on her desk. "I've got a lot of work to do before Monday. Can this wait?"

"Well, not really, Loraine," I said in my sweetest voice. "You see, I still have to find out who murdered Willie."

"Do you have any information?" she asked, going back to her work.

"Well, yes I might. We got the lab report back and we know how Willie died. It was oleander poisoning."

Perhaps the only indication that she heard what I said is that the mechanical pencil in her hand snapped in half. Still, I was a trained detective and I notice these little things, especially since it sounded like a firecracker going off.

"So do you know anything about that?" I asked innocently.

"Why would I know anything?" her voice rasped.

"Apparently, JJ was mixing up a concoction in the kitchen for some...mmm...pests. She was using oleander leaves."

"So you think JJ did it?"

"No. JJ didn't do it. But she mentioned that you were with her in the kitchen."

"No, I don't remember that," she obviously lied, her eyes dropping back to the papers in front of her.

"Well, JJ remembers it pretty well," I said, still sweetly. "I don't think she'd forget something like that."

"I said I don't remember. That's all," she said dismissively, waving me out without looking up.

I closed the door behind me, wondering what she was up to. She was guilty as original sin and in this up to her ears, but I still didn't know her role in the drama. Shoot. I didn't even know all the players. Did she kill Willie Boyd? Maybe. Could I prove it? Not yet.

As usual, the first Sunday of Advent fell on the first Sunday in December. The first Sunday of Advent was actually the closest Sunday to the Feast of St. Andrew, which was on November twenty-eighth and marked the beginning of the church year. It was our custom to begin the season of Advent with the Great Litany chanted in procession and led by the priest. We only dragged the thurible and the incense out of the closet a couple of times a year, but this was the big one. All the smells and bells as they say in the biz.

Herself had not ever practiced chanting the Great Litany and this was her first Advent processional at St. Barnabas. When I mentioned to her, on Sunday morning before the service, that I'd be happy to go over it with her—a magnanimous gesture on my part, I thought—her reply was smug and to the point.

"I'll just let the Holy Spirit take care of it."

"Why don't you give me ten minutes of rehearsal and we'll let the Holy Spirit worry about something else this morning," I fired back.

She didn't take the hint. Added to the fun of the procession was the sound of bells being rung around and about the church and a cloud of smoke from the incense pot that would do credit to the Santiago de Compostela. I—yes, even I—think they may have overfilled the incense pot just a tad.

The man in charge of the incense was our resident thurifer

Benny Dawkins and he, unlike the current priest, took his job very seriously. He began practicing in September, diligently getting the hang of swinging the smoking thurible. He would start slowly with a straight swing which he called the Tallulah Bankhead in honor of the sardonic actress's famous quote "Dahlin', your gown looks fabulous, but your purse in on fire." The rest of September would be spent perfecting the Big Ben and the Cross Your Heart. He'd practice every day in October until he had finely honed the Around the World and the very difficult Walk the Dog. In November he put the final touches on his ultimate maneuver, the Doubly-Inverted Reverse Swan, which he had only attempted once in public and where he, unfortunately, had knocked out poor Iona Hoskins when the heavy, smoking pot caught her behind the left ear and set her wig on fire. Other than that one incident, which many in the congregation viewed as a blessing due to the change in Iona's attitude after the accident, Benny had an unblemished record, in services as well as in competition. At the International Thurifer Invitational in London, he entered in the Singles, No Side-Boat division and was awarded second place for the tricks portion of the event, a highly respectable third in freestyle and won the Bronze medal in the overall, losing only to the legendary Alaister Hewish from Yorkminster and an upstart wunderkind from St. Thomaskirche in Leipzig. Benny would incorporate all his signature moves and several improvisations into his procession, all the while walking in strict time, looking straight ahead and never losing a grain of incense. It was a pleasure to watch him work.

Mother Ryan took a big breath to begin the procession. The Great Litany is a rather long recitation and apparently the Holy Spirit wasn't helping her out: she was lost before the first paragraph was finished. Then she panicked and started hyperventilating. I could tell this, as could the rest of the congregation, because she was walking right behind Benny and when she started to gasp for breath, what she got was smoke—and a lot of it.

The smoke that burning incense produces is very pungent and is manufactured that way purposely so the fragrance will carry throughout the nave of the church, following the old testament edict "Let my prayers rise as incense." On this, the first Sunday of Advent, the smoke to rector ratio was very high.

As soon as Herself inhaled a billowing cloud of smoke, I knew she was finished with the "Great Litany in Procession." As she started choking, Elaine, who was leading the choir behind her, sat her down in the end seat of one of the pews. I immediately took over, chanting the text from the balcony as the thurifer, the crucifer, and the choir made their way around the church. It was a pretty good transition and the only people who noticed anything amiss were the choir—and they were used to changing horses in the middle of the stream.

"She turned green pretty quickly," Elaine told me afterward. "I would call the color somewhere between 'Julep Ice' and 'Frogbelly Mint.'" Elaine took pride in her interior decorating skills.

Herself managed to get through the first part of the service once the procession was over. I noticed that her sermon was shorter than usual and she didn't really get any of her normal color back. Still, I thought she might make it to the end of the service. I was wrong.

It was the communion ritual that finished her off. She managed to get through the liturgy, but when she had to drink the wine, it was more than her queasy stomach could endure. She left the Lay Eucharistic Ministers to administer the bread and wine to the congregation, and quickly disappeared behind the hidden door into the sacristy. I was beginning to play something appropriate for communion when I detected the first hint of what will probably become one of the legendary services in the history of St. Barnabas.

The control board for the sound system at the church was located up in the choir loft. Down in front were two reading microphones on the lecterns and a wireless mike—what we called the "walkin' mike"—clipped to the rector's frock and turned off and on at his or her discretion by means of a toggle switch on the battery pack. Unfortunately for Loraine Ryan, she had left the toggle on.

I looked up at Bob Solomon, one of the basses, who was nearest the amplifier. The rest of the choir was heading down for communion and he was the last to leave. My eyebrows arched as I continued to play, asking the wordless question. There, in front of him as he looked down, clearly marked, was the dial on the amp that would silence the walkin' mike. He looked back at me and smiled with an innocence belying his black heart, patted the amplifier affectionately, gazed briefly toward heaven as if asking forgiveness, and followed the rest of the choir, closing the door to the choir loft behind him.

Mercifully, it didn't last too long. But most of the parishioners will never forget hearing, as they knelt to receive the sacrament on that first Sunday of Advent, "The gifts of God for the people of God."

"Hurrrrraaachhh!"

"Take in remembrance…"

"Urrrrallllccch!"

"And feed in your heart by faith…"

"urrgh…"

"with thanksgiving."

"Bluhreaaaarch!"

Six weeks after the murder and Megan was still on the case.

"What about the 911 tape? Have you forgotten about that?"

I was chopping some chives for our salad. I had some pork chops on the grill outside, but they would be working for another half hour or so.

"No, I haven't forgotten about the tape. I have a copy right here somewhere," I said, pointing with my knife to a pile of debris which was creeping across the sideboard like so much administrative kudzu. "I just haven't listened to it for a while."

"Well, put it in the player."

"Then you have to finish the salad."

I handed her the knife and rummaged around in the papers until I came up with the copy of the tape. Then I turned off the Monteverdi *Vespers Service,* which had been gracing our pre-luncheon revelry, and dropped the cassette into the player.

It was a woman's timbre, all right, but deeper than it should have been, with a hollow sound like someone disguising her voice.

"I'd like to report a dead man. He's in the choir loft at St. Barnabas Church in St. Germaine." Click. It played four more times. I had dubbed it over and over so I wouldn't have to rewind the tape.

Meg stopped chopping and sat at the table with a cup of luke-warm coffee, listening intently to the voice.

"It sure sounds familiar. Can't you send this tape to the forensic voice lab and get an analysis done? Then you could listen to it with the technician, and he can tweak the speed and pitch until it sounds just like the killer who you will recognize immediately. That's what they would do on TV."

"This is St. Germaine, not New York," I said. "We don't have a voice lab. I would wager that there is no voice lab in the entire state of North Carolina. In fact, there may be no such thing as a forensic voice lab. I certainly have never seen one."

"Well then," she sniffed. "I'm sure you're right. There's probably no such thing."

"Well, what if we just sped the tape up a little? Would that make you happy?" I asked, trying to humor her, but holding out little hope that anything we might be able to do would produce a usable clue.

Meg perked right back up. "Yes it would. How can we do it?"

I sighed with audible resignation. "Give me a minute and I'll dump it onto the computer."

"Great," said Meg as she got up and attacked the salad with gusto. "This will be finished in short order."

I fired up my iBook, found the requisite jacks to attach the cassette to the firewire port and dumped the fifteen second sound bite onto the hard drive. With a sound design program that I generally use for live recording, I could now speed up the 911 call, slow it down, change the pitch—just about anything they could do in one of those mythical New York forensic voice labs.

I unhooked the iBook and brought it over to the table, where Meg was dishing up the salads.

"Here we are, madam. Your private voice lab."

"Neat. OK, play it," she said.

I hit the play button.

"I'd like to report a dead man. He's in the choir loft at St. Barnabas Church in St. Germaine."

"It's harder to hear on those little computer speakers," Meg complained. "Can you hook the computer up to the stereo?"

"Your wish is my command. It'll take just a second."

Meg took the opportunity to fetch us both a glass of cabernet. By the time she was finished pouring, the computer was hooked up and ready.

"I'd like to report a dead man," the computer said.

"OK, let's speed it up just a bit," said Meg, listening intently.

I bumped the speed by fifty percent and listened to a high-pitched, brassy voice say, "I'd wike to weport a dead man."

"It was TWEETY BIRD!" I exclaimed. "I knew I'd heard that voice before."

"Oh, haha," she said. "Take it back to about ten."

This time it was more like Barbara Walters.

"You know," Meg said "I didn't notice it before at normal speed, but she has a bit of a lisp. That's why she sounds like Tweety."

"You're right," I said, suddenly interested. I played it again.

"OK, can you leave it at ten and stretch the time back to the original."

"Well," I said, realizing I wasn't getting any salad until we were finished, "I can do it sort of backwards. I can take the original clip, make sure the length stays constant and then raise the pitch ten cents."

"Ten cents?"

"That's recording lingo. You can raise the pitch an entire step or any number of cents up to one hundred."

"OK. Is ten cents enough?"

"I've saved the original, so we can play around with this one."

We tried ten cents, then twenty, then thirty. At thirty-seven, Meg said "Stop. That's it. I know that voice."

I nodded. "Yep. Me too."

"Some detective. Why didn't you do this six weeks ago?"

"Sheesh. I didn't even know I had a forensic voice lab till you told me. I'll talk to our suspect first thing tomorrow morning. And it's not like I don't have anything to do. My plate is full. It's the height of the leaf season and the tourists, as usual, are howling at the moon. Most of the problems are double parking, shoplifting and traffic violations, but get this. On Friday, a woman came into the station and complained to Nancy that the night clerk at the Roadway had sold her baking powder instead of cocaine. She wanted to file a complaint. She even gave Nancy the baggie of powder."

Meg looked at me in disbelief. "Was it baking powder?"

"Nope. It was cocaine all right. We drove her down to Boone. Told her she needed to file her complaint from the courthouse. About halfway there, she started getting scared and told us she'd decided not to press charges. Anyway, they booked her on possession and locked her up."

Meg shook her head and giggled aloud. "What about the night clerk?"

"On my list for tomorrow. I don't have any direct evidence he was dealing, but I'm going to put the fear of God in him."

"Are you going to save the file?" she asked, glancing at the computer.

"Done," I said, hitting the save keys. "And now, Miss Marple. *Now* may I satisfy my gnawing appetite?"

"You bet, Sugarpie," she said with a smile as she leaned across the table and gave me a long, delicious kiss of the mind-numbing variety. "Or would you rather have the salad?"

Chapter 10

Amber Dawn, the bishop's personal trainer and a vocal
performance major in college, handed me the latest PCD
that I was in charge of implementing. No wonder the alto
in tweed was ticked as last season's Beagle-of-the-Month.
Amber wasn't the brightest bulb on the Christmas tree and
she sure didn't know much about music. Yeah, I admit it. I
had had a fling with her. Who wouldn't? But eventually
you've got to have more than a drop-dead gorgeous body
and a face that Aphrodite would envy.

"Amber," I said, lighting up a cigar after a particularly memorable tussle. "What is your opinion on the rise
of homophony in the classical era?"

"Hmmm," said Amber Dawn, Personal Trainer, screwing up
her beautiful brow and thinking as hard as she had during
the finals of the Miss Poke Salad Beauty Pageant--an
official Miss America preliminary competition. "I think that
it's an irrational fear," she said, after some deliberation.
"What they do in the privacy of their own homes is their
own business."

"Amber," I asked hopefully. "What are your discerning
notions about the use of augmentation in the soprano voice
as an essential element of the Baroque fugue?"

"Honey," she squeaked. "I think if those sopranos want
to wear falsettos, more power to 'em."

I vowed to break up with her then and there, but
before I got the chance, the Bishop picked up her option
and I was last week's headlines. Still, I think she had a
soft spot left in one or two ventricles for an aging detective.

We entered the tavern arm in arm and I offered her a
stool at the bar. Before I could order a couple of drinks,
the guy sitting next to her was already making a move. It
always happened.

"Hi baby. What's your sign?"

"Hello there," she replied, positioning her abundant bosom for the utmost effect and batting her eyelashes as if she was trying to achieve free flight. "I'm a Libretto."

I was outta there.

On Monday morning I was at the church bright and early—early for me being around 9:00. Herself was a manic frenzy of activity. Her conference was set to begin the following afternoon with opening services at five followed by a seminar and a get-acquainted coffee time afterwards. The altar guild was in high gear in the sacristy and the sanctuary trying to follow her bellowed commands. Rhiza Walker was following her around with a clipboard doing her best to take notes.

"Hayden," she spit. "You have got to get busy on your service music. I left it up on the organ for you. God, this altar guild is full of idiots. I keep telling them that we don't need the communion wine and the wafers. Our services utilize the 'milk and honey' ritual. Honestly, I don't know how Father Brown got anything done around here. Of course," she added, "he never hosted a conference of this magnitude. What are you playing tomorrow?"

"Well, I've been meaning to talk to you about that. I'm really pretty busy this week."

"Whaaat?!!" she shrieked. "You've known about this conference for months!"

"Yes, and for months, I've told you I would be busy," I replied over my shoulder as I left the sacristy and entered the sanctuary.

Beverly Greene and Liz Newhart were working on the altar flowers. Liz greeted me as I came in. Beverly smiled at me, nodded and continued working on the arrangement.

"Hi, Hayden," Liz said. "Good to see you. The choir sounded great yesterday. The rest of the service was...interesting," she said giggling, and looking around to see if Herself was coming in behind me unnoticed.

"We do our best," I said humbly.

"Are you here to practice for the service? We'd love to listen."

"Nope. I'm here to see Beverly."

Beverly looked up at me, startled, her blue eyes wide.

I smiled at her. "Can we talk in my office?"

She nodded but didn't say anything, put the vase down and followed me out of the sanctuary and up the stairs.

I didn't use my office for much. I had a few vestments, a couple of chairs, a desk and some books. The office was situated in the old organ pipe chamber above the front of the nave. When the organ was moved from the front of the church to the rear loft, the pipe chamber became a perfect alcove for my small sanctuary. I opened the door and ushered Beverly in.

"Have a seat," I offered.

"No thanks. I think I'll stand."

I pulled out a pocket tape player, set it on the desk and pushed the "play" button.

"I'd like to report a dead man. He's in the choir loft at St. Barnabas Church in St. Germaine," the tape said at its originally recorded speed.

"Would you know anything about this?" I asked Beverly, who was chewing on her bottom lip.

"No."

I had left the tape playing. "I'd like to report a dead man. He's in the choir loft at St. Barnabas Church in St. Germaine," said the tape again, now at a higher pitch and slowed down slightly—the recording as altered by the computer. There was no mistake. It was Beverly's voice.

She sank into a chair. "What did you do? Send it to the forensic voice lab?" she asked, resignation apparent in her question.

I clicked the tape off. "Where is this forensic voice lab I've been hearing so much about? Everyone knows about it except me."

"I don't know. I just assumed we had one."

"Back to the recording," I continued. "It was you that made the 911 call. Why didn't you tell me?"

"I didn't think it was important."

"You tried to disguise your voice."

"Well...um...yes, I did. I didn't want to get involved. I thought it was just an accident."

I leaned up against my desk and folded my arms across my chest—in my opinion, my most authoritative, professional pose. "Tell me what happened."

She paused for a moment as if to gather her thoughts, or to resurrect a well-rehearsed statement—I couldn't tell which.

"I was here that Friday afternoon. Georgia had come in early to fix communion because she couldn't be here on Saturday morning when we usually do it."

"I remember."

"I was in the sacristy at about five o'clock arranging the flowers for Sunday. I was in the back here by the sink when Willie came in. I didn't say anything to him 'cause he gives...uh...gave me the creeps. I just kept quiet."

"Can you be sure about the time?"

"It must have been a little bit after five or so. I remember because I heard the bells chime five, so it was after that."

"5:10?"

"Probably close to that," she said. I decided that she actually was trying to remember. Her story wasn't quite tight enough to have been rehearsed.

"Willie came into the sacristy through the alley door. I guess he'd come from the kitchen. He walked over to the phone, looked up a number in the phone book and dialed. He said something about wine being missing and fixing a lock, but he didn't talk very long, and I didn't hear everything he said."

"Did he have anything with him?"

"A bottle of communion wine. One of the big ones. I thought he was swiping it, but I didn't want to say anything. There might have been another explanation, and I didn't want to get him in trouble."

"Did he leave after the phone call?" I asked.

She bit her lower lip again. "He did something very weird," she said. I nodded at her to continue.

"He went over to the closet where the priest and the communion servers keep their vestments."

"That closet's kept locked, isn't it?"

"Yes it is, but Willie had a key. He opened the closet door, slid the robes around for a second and pulled out a cross. It looked like Mother Ryan's cross. You know, the one made of olive wood that she got in the Holy Land."

I remembered the cross. Herself had made quite a big deal out of consecrating it during a Sunday morning service when she brought it back from her pilgrimage. It also occurred to me that she hadn't worn it since Willie was killed.

"Then what?"

She hesitated. "He...um...."

"What happened, Bev?" I asked her sternly, my patience starting to wear.

"He kissed the cross and put it in his pocket. He didn't see me," she said quickly and softly.

"He kissed it?" I asked. "How did he kiss it?"

"Well, you know," she added, now embarrassed. "He held it up sort of in front of his lips and he kissed it." She paused. "It was a long kiss. He closed his eyes."

"A long kiss?"

"I don't know how to explain it exactly, but it was creepy." Her eyes went to the floor. "And that wasn't the first time he'd taken it."

I waited for her to explain.

"He'd taken it before. Mother Ryan caught him at least once putting the cross in his pocket. And a couple of times it was missing, but then showed up a few days later. I don't know why she didn't just give it to him."

"OK, then what happened?"

She looked up again. "He locked the closet door back and went out the sacristy door into the church."

"Did he take the wine with him?"

"Yeah. He took it. I forgot."

"Beverly, why didn't you tell me all this before?"

"I couldn't tell you."

"Why not?" I persisted.

"If I *do* tell you, will you promise not to arrest me?" She looked into my eyes and I could tell she was quite serious.

"I can't promise you that," I said. "But I will try to talk the judge into a minimum sentence. Just tell me the problem and we'll work it out."

Her shoulders tensed as she readied her confession. "I was called for jury duty that morning in Boone, but I told them that I had made a doctor's appointment at the Mayo Clinic in Rochester six months ago that I couldn't reschedule. So they let me off."

My laugh could have been heard in the jury room.

"It's not funny!" she exclaimed. "They'll throw me in jail. You can't just skip jury duty."

"Did you write the note I found on the organ?" I asked, knowing the answer.

"What note?"

Yep.

After I got back to the office, I phoned Kent Murphee at the coroner's office.

"Hi, Kent, this is Hayden Konig."

"Hayden! How're you doing?"

"I'm just fine. Listen, I've got a question for you."

"Shoot."

"You remember Willie Boyd?"

"The oleander poisoning? Sure, I remember."

"Did he have anything in his pockets when he was brought in?"

"I don't remember. Hang on a sec."

I heard the rustling of papers and hoped that Dr. Murphee was a little more organized in his professional life than I was.

"Got it," he said, coming back on the phone. "Let's see...here it is. A bottle cap from a Red Dog beer, a ring of keys, a wallet with various business cards, three dollars, a library card and his driver's license, forty-three cents in change and a wooden cross on a chain."

"No kidding? A library card?" I was surprised. "What happened to all that stuff?"

"We sent it back with Mr. Boyd."

"To the funeral home?"

"Yeah. No one claimed it."

"Thanks, Kent. You have a fine day. Oh, and if I don't see you again before the Yuletide season begins, have a Merry Christmas."

"You do the same. Bye."

My next call was to Swallow's Mortuary in Boone, the outfit that had seen to Willie's burial.

"Mr. Swallow, please."

"Speaking," came back a low, gravelly bass voice straight out of a Dickens novel.

"Mr. Swallow, this is Detective Konig from St. Germaine."

"Yes sir, how may I help you?"

"You made the arrangements to have a Willie Boyd interred here in St. Germaine about six weeks ago."

"I remember."

"When he was sent over to the mortuary from the coroner's office, were his effects sent with him?" I asked.

"That is usually the case."

"I need to look at those personal effects."

"Well," said Mr. Swallow. "Let me check my records." He must have had them close at hand because it wasn't more than a few seconds before he was back on the phone.

"We sent Mr. Boyd's effects to St. Barnabas Church in St. Germaine."

"St. Barnabas?" I asked.

"The church was paying for the funeral and there was no next-of-kin. It seemed the prudent thing to do."

"Thanks for your help, That should take care of it."

"One more thing," Mr. Swallow added before he hung up the phone. "He had a wooden cross."

"Yes?"

"I placed it in his hands myself before we sealed the coffin. I thought it would be a comfort to him."

I phoned Judge Adams in Boone and got a court order to open Willie's coffin. We would dig Willie back up on Wednesday morning. I didn't think he'd mind. Then I stopped by the church office.

"Marilyn?" I asked. "Did we get a package from Swallow's with Willie Boyd's belongings?"

"We got a package. I didn't open it though."

"Where'd you put it?"

"It's in the kitchen pantry I think. I didn't know what to do with it."

"That's great. Thanks," I said, heading out the door with the kitchen in sight.

I found the package in the kitchen pantry just where Marilyn said it would be. I opened it up and dumped Willie's effects onto the counter. In front of me, on the stainless steel counter, was a bottle cap, Willie's wallet and library card, some change and his ring of keys. I picked up the keys and looked at them carefully. Then I took them over to the wine closet and, not finding the old skeleton key on the ring, reached into my pocket and returned the missing closet key to Willie's collection.

Later that afternoon I got a call from the bishop.

"Hello Hayden," he said in a vacuous baritone. "This is Bishop Douglas."

"Well, hello George. Good to talk to you." It always irked him when I called him George, which is probably why I continued to do it.

"Listen Hayden, I'll get right to the point. Loraine Ryan has called my office three times in the last two hours to complain that you won't play the organ for her Women's Conference. I want you to get over to St. Barnabas right now. Don't give her any more trouble."

"Do you have any idea what kind of services she's planning?"

"It's a conference for women in the ministry. I presume the services are from the prayerbook."

"Well, George," I explained gently, my ire rising. "These services are definitely *not* from the Book of Common Prayer. And not that I am accountable to the diocesan office, but since we are on a first-name basis, I will offer you this purview of my inexplicable actions. Firstly, I'm an employee of the church only for insurance purposes. I take no salary. My compensation is put back into the music department's trust account which is managed by the music committee—not the church. That being said, I will play for whomever and whatever I want, and I would no sooner play the organ for those wacko services than I would give a recital of Christy Lane's Greatest Hits. Now I suppose the church could replace me, but I doubt that they will."

"Ah. Well, I didn't understand the situation."

"Yes. Well, now you do. Bye, George."

"Hayden, just a min—" Click.

My, but that was satisfying.

I wanted to see Meg that evening and fill her in on the recent developments, but she was off to the Biltmore Estate in Asheville with her mother to view the Christmas festivities. So Monday night I was home alone with a couple of Cubans—*Romeo and Julietta*—some Blanchet's Single Barrel Bourbon and J. S. Bach's *Magnificat* and *Christmas Oratorio*. Three hours of Baroque bliss.

Tuesday morning found me at The Slab. I generally met Nancy and Dave for breakfast on Monday to have our departmental meeting and hit the highlights of the week ahead but Nancy had been under the weather and I had business to attend to. So it was Tuesday. On this glorious morning, Pete was acting as waiter, cook, cashier and host due to the flu bug that had laid low his help. Luckily for him, we were the only ones in the café.

"I hope it hasn't been too busy," I joked, as he brought the dishes to our table.

"It was a bit hectic around eight, but I just told Louise and Carlton they had to make their own breakfasts. They jumped right in."

"And paid you for the privilege, I'll bet."

"Yep. And left a tip to boot," Pete said, pulling up a chair. "Dave, get me some coffee, will you?"

Dave laughed and got up to bring the pot over to the table.

"You know," I said. "If this is an *Official Meeting...*"

"I can't afford any more of your *Official Meetings*," Pete broke in. "Let's just say I'm sitting in as an interested party—and as such, would there happen to be any developments in the Boyd case that I can pass on to the council? It's still on the 'old business' portion of the agenda."

"We were just going to talk about that," said Nancy, attacking her pancakes with gusto. "It would be a shame to let these get cold though."

"Good point," I said, picking up my fork.

We polished off the major portion of our breakfasts in short order. Pete made another pot of coffee and I pulled out my list.

"OK, first on the agenda is the Boyd case."

Dave was pouring his fourth cup of coffee. "It's really the *only* thing on our agenda."

"Not so," I replied. "Don't forget the Christmas parade and the Living Crèche on the eighteenth. We've got to get the street closed and hire a couple of guys from Boone to help us with the traffic."

"I'll take care of that," said Nancy, twirling the last bit of pancake through the remaining maple syrup on her plate like an imaginary ice skater doing a triple toe loop before popping it into her mouth.

"I thought the Supreme Court decided that live manger scenes in public places were against the law," Dave said. "Wasn't it some sort of ACLU case?"

Pete broke in. "The *hell* with that! If we can't have a goddamn manger scene, what's the point of Christmas?"

"Elegantly and succinctly put," I said, hiding a smile. "I presume that the Rotary Club is still in charge of the event."

"I think this is the year that Kiwanis does the parade and Rotary does the crèche," Pete said. "I'm pretty sure that last year Rotary did the parade."

"Dave, will you check with Bob Solomon? He's the president of the Rotary. Who's in charge of Kiwanis?"

"Marta Jenkins," Pete said.

"And check with Marta about the parade," I said to Dave who was diligently taking notes. "They should have everything all planned out, but we'll still have to touch base with them. We need to know starting times, who's in charge, their contact people...anything else?" I asked.

"I don't think so. I'll check on everything," Dave said. "If something else comes up, I'll let you know."

"Now," I said, pulling my tattered list from my pocket. "Let's see where we are. You understand, Pete, that this is all highly confidential."

"Of course, of course."

"OK, here's what we know," I began.

"Are you still using that list?" said Nancy, pointing at it with her pancake laden fork and dripping syrup irreverently across the top of the page, disgust evident in her voice. "I'm really getting embarrassed for you, Hayden. You're *supposed* to be a professional."

"Quiet, you. I'm the boss," I said, as I began reviewing my list.

When?

Willie Boyd was killed on a Friday afternoon. 5:12 p.m.—give or take. JJ saw him around five as he passed through the kitchen. And Beverly Green saw him at 5:10 making a phone call to police. He then went up to the choir loft where he had a drink and expired. He stole the wine earlier that afternoon, hid the cases of wine in the trunk of his car and drank from one of the bottles that he took to the choir loft. However, the wine wasn't poisoned.

Who?

There seems to have been a witness and there's a possible clue in the form of a cryptic note. I was pretty sure the clue was genuine.

I saw who did it. It's Him. It's Matthew.
O hark the herald angels sing;
The boy's descent which lifted up the world.

All the Matthews (first and last names) in the county have alibis. It's the last line that puzzles me. We're still working on it. JJ was the one cooking up the oleander broth. Mother Ryan was in the kitchen with her, but claimed not to remember. What is her reason? I think she's still the key.

Why?

I had a new theory. I think that Willie's death was an accident. It was a murder all right, but it was the wrong murder. If this is the case, there may be another.

How?

Oleander poisoning. But it wasn't found in Willie's stomach. The poison entered his system through his mouth, absorbed though the oral membranes, but was not swallowed. I suspected it was Mother Ryan's olive wood cross that did him in. We wouldn't know until Wednesday when we disinterred Willie.

"What about 'What?'" asked Dave.

"What what?" I asked.

"You know. When, who, why, how and what. *That* what."

"Shut up, Dave."

At 4:45 the church was abuzz with "wimmyn" priests and reporters. I sneaked up to the choir loft to watch the opening service. I didn't turn on the lights however, preferring to remain a shadowy specter. There, sitting in the dark, were Elaine Hixon, Beverly Greene and Georgia Wester.

"Shhh," they hushed me as a group. I locked the choir loft door behind me. "No sense inviting trouble," I said as I took off my coat and hat and sat in a chair against the back window. Looking down at the back of the congregation's heads, I tried to pick out which of our own flock had decided to engage in these liturgical shenanigans. I recognized Rhiza and Malcolm Walker right away. He was the Senior Warden and expected to attend. They had 'their' pew, of course, which they always sat in and were easy to find. Rhiza's golden locks always seemed to shimmer. JJ was in attendance, as was most of the altar guild. Bob Solomon and his wife Sandra were sitting back a bit, away from the action. There were a few others, but definitely not a huge swell of support from our own congregation.

The service began with all the wimmyn in their finest priestly regalia, gathering around the altar, which had been moved out front to make room for the celebration. The priests circled the altar, joined hands—all except two of them who began playing hand drums of African origin, and started a low hum. One of them, the featured speaker of the conference and, I presumed, the "celebrant" for this evening's event, began speaking.

"Here we taste, see and savor how good it is to be in our bodies."

The beat of the drums got louder and more insistent.

"As we ReImagine God in our feminine image, please speak aloud any name for God that you wish to use," said Herself, hands raised, filled with glory. A number of flashes went off as reporters took advantage of the photo op which had obviously arranged in defiance of the St. Barnabas edit against flash photography during a service of *any* kind.

From the circle of women came new names for the deity.

"Moon Mother," said one woman with a Boston accent.

"Sophia," said another.

"Mary," offered the third.

A pause; the drums and the humming; then Mother Ryan.

"That's wonderful. Any others?"

"Wanda."

I'm sure my snort was audible because the three ladies in the balcony spun around and glared at me before turning their attention back to the show.

"Wanda?" I whispered.

"Shhh."

Each womyn had taken a glass of milk mixed with honey off the table. Now they sang together "Sophia, Creator God, let your milk and honey flow. Shower us with your love."

"Our maker Sophia, we are wimmyn in your image. With the hot blood of our wombs we give form to new life," sang the celebrant.

"Our mother Sophia, we are wimmyn in your image. With the milk of our breasts we suckle the children," sang Herself.

After each verse came the refrain from all the women "Sophia, Sophia, Sophia, shower us with your love."

"Our guide Sophia. With our moist mouths we kiss away a tear. With the honey of wisdom in our mouths we prophesy to all peoples."

At this they all drank their honeyed milk.

"O Sophia, goddess of Wisdom, you are a lamp unto our feet and a light unto our path."

"O Moon Mother...Wanda...goddess of Creation, we enter into community which strengthens and renews us."

They all sang together "Bless us now and dream the vision, share the wisdom dwelling deep within."

When the "milk and honey" service had concluded, the wimmyn had a period of brief announcements before the evening service began. It followed the standard Evening Prayer service pretty closely with all the music accompanied by an electronic keyboard played by one of the priests. The anthem was a piece titled *As God Is Our Mother* on a text by Hildegard von Bingen, the twelfth-century mystic. They had rehearsed it earlier in the afternoon and it wasn't very difficult. I know this because I wrote it.

The anthem was written about two years ago for a competition that invited women composers to submit an anthem utilizing a text by a prominent woman poet. I sent it in under the name Dame Marjorie Wallace. It didn't win. At least I never saw any prize money. The reason it didn't win, I figured, was probably because of the fictional biography of Dame Marjorie that I wrote to accompany it. When I opened the service bulletin I almost choked on the cigar I had been chomping angrily since the milk and honey ceremony.

Our anthem this evening, "As God Is Our Mother,"
is by the esteemed composer Dame Marjorie Wallace.
Dame Marjorie has had an interesting and varied

career. First coming to national prominence as a member of the 1968 British Olympic Bicycling Team, she also held a position as one of the Queen Mother's premier hat makers, stunning the fashion world with her bold and innovative hat designs. She retired from Haberdashery after losing her left leg in a horrible accident involving a terrorist attack on the Queen Mother in the form of an exploding hat wren—one of the stuffed birds her employer insisted on decorating her hats with in the early 1970's.

Not being able to perform her duties due to psychological implications involving a newly formed diagnosis of explodornithophobia, she took her disability pension and turned her considerable talents toward music composition and bassoon playing and immigrated to Canada. Long an advocate of wimmyn's rights, she incorporated her love of art and bicycling with her culinary expertise and opened the first bicycle shop/tea room in North America. She subsequently founded a feminist artists' community in 1972 in Saskatchewan called Lesbian Actors, Composers, Tea and Truffle Enterprises (LACTATE). Her ambitions in the choral arts saw the founding of the wimmyn's chorale "Lactate Dominum."

Dame Marjorie, along with being a composer of considerable note, is also the inventor of the "monoped" bicycle and holds several international patents. She lives with her long time companion and life-partner, Ms. Alice Carpenter.

I got to my feet after the anthem, went down the stairs, out the front doors and onto the lawn. Bev, Elaine and Georgia joined me a few moments later closing the doors behind them.

"Isn't that the piece you wrote last year? We sang it in the choir," said Elaine.

"I don't remember," I said with a grin. "It sounded familiar though."

"Are you going to tell them?" asked Beverly.

"I think not."

Just then the front doors opened and the wimmyn processed out the front doors of the church to the sound of drums, bells and finger cymbals, the conclave of reporters and onlookers following closely. We ducked around the corner of the church, keeping the group in sight.

As the drums became silent, Herself raised her hands, resplendent in the fluorescent glow of the streetlight, and said, "Together we have given birth to a ReImagining Community that extends to every corner of our world."

The drums and cymbals began anew with restored vigor to the refrain "Sophia, Sophia, Sophia, shower us with your love." As they chanted together, their collective voices straining to a frenzied pitch, suddenly one of the womyn screamed and pointed to the sky. They all glanced heavenward and there, framed by the full moon which was still low in the sky, was the goddess Sophia herself. She hung there for a just moment, transfixed in naked beauty, before drifting into a power pole and landing against a transformer.

The resulting explosion and shower of fire that rained down on the wimmyn priests was enough to convert most of them back to orthodox Christianity. Four of them checked into the hospital with "severe emotional distress." Six got into their cars and went home immediately. The goddess Sophia met her untimely end amid the fragrance of electrical conflagration and burning latex.

The girls and I just stood and watched with disbelief.

"The Lord works in mysterious ways," said Georgia thoughtfully, "but Arlen won't be very happy."

The transformer was totally destroyed and electricity in a two-block area was out for two days until another one was installed.

The church was closed and the rest of the *ReImagining God*

the Mother in the Twenty-First Century conference was moved to Greensboro. The reporters went home and the pictures never made the local papers. I figured that was the Bishop's doing.

Chapter 11

Visions of Amber Dawn, Personal Trainer, melted away like Brie in an Episcopalian's microwave as the alto currently in my office stood and swept the shotgun across my desk.

"That's enough reminiscing," she said, breathing hard, the buttons on her tweed vest straining to the bursting point. "I want answers and I want them now."

"Well, ask me the questions and I'll sing like Pavoratti in a lasagna factory."

She slumped back into the chair, the wind going out of her ample sails and her buttons breathing an audible sigh of relief.

"It's the Bishop."

I nodded. It was always the Bishop.

"He's gotten a judge to put a restraining order on our publishing company."

"Why would he do that?" I asked feigning interest. I was still more interested in the shotgun.

"We were going into production of our latest product. A new series of Scratch-N-Sniff Anthems."

Now I was interested and I perked up quick as Mrs. Olsen's septic tank as Denver Tweed went into her marketing spiel. She pulled out a sheet of paper and started reading.

"We understand, psychologically speaking, that certain responses are triggered within our subconscious by either visual, aural or olfactory memories. That is--sight, sound or smell. And this is precisely why we were about to introduce this new product, which we think will be quickly adopted by all concerned congregations."

I nodded. I could see where she was going with this. I mean, who wouldn't want to be singing "O Tannenbaum" and actually be able to smell the scent of the piney woods? Or

"Lo, How A Rose" while the familiar odor of rose petals wafts through the air. And this was only scratching the surface, so to speak.

I let her rattle on without interruption. Denver wasn't smart enough to have come up with this on her own. It was a brilliant idea but I knew why the Bishop quashed it. They hadn't included the mandatory clerical kickback in her business plan. If the Bishop didn't get a piece of the money pie, the pie never got near the oven.

"What happened to Isabel Gerhardt?" Meg asked. "You know, the soprano from Chapter 5. And Amber Dawn?"

"Oh yeah. I forgot about Isabel. Amber's still around I think. The problem is that my characters keep wandering off. Do you suppose it's because they're jealous of my writing prowess?"

"No. As a writer, you stink. So far you have three women in this story and no one seems to know what's going on. There's no plot and no continuity," she complained.

"Look, I'll try to tie everything together."

"Please do."

The owl showed up on Tuesday night. It was a good omen, I thought, but I didn't know of what just yet. We walked in and Meg spotted it at once—in the window over the sink, almost translucent in the moonlight. The young white barn owl, not yet fully grown, was peering intently into the house with a mouse dangling from his beak. We sat quietly at the table, and as we watched him, careful not to make any sudden movements; he tossed the mouse up, caught it by the head and swallowed it in two bites. Then, after preening his feathers to our utter delight, he launched himself in a flurry of motion and was gone into the darkness.

"What was that about?" asked Meg, as if I had an answer.

"I don't know. I hope he comes back though."

"Me too," she said. "That was cool."

At the gravesite, the backhoe was at work, carefully removing the still loose earth from the lid of Willie Boyd's final resting place. Mr. Swallow, the backhoe operator and one of Swallow's minions named Bill were here to do the dirty work. Nancy and I were here as witnesses and to pick up the article in question. As the top of Willie's vault came into view, Bill jumped into the hole with a flat shovel and cleaned the remaining dirt off the steel covering that kept water off the coffin. Working quickly, he and the backhoe operator, who had found a shovel of his own, removed the remaining earth from the grave, giving themselves room to slide a couple of nylon straps past the blocks and under the floor of the vault. While Bill attached the straps together, making a sling to lift the vault out of the hole, his partner swung the backhoe around, presenting the front-end loader for the heavy lifting. Bill hooked the straps to the bucket and the hydraulic monster lifted the vault out of the grave with no apparent effort. During the entire process, Mr. Swallow, dressed in his immaculate black suit, stood silently, his hands pressed together as if in prayer, with no expression crossing his visage.

"It shouldn't be long now," I said to Nancy, who had been strangely quiet during the whole process. "We're almost there."

Little Willie, silk and sashes
Fell in the fire and was burned to ashes,
Now even when the room grows chilly,
We haven't the heart to poke up Willie.

It was an old poem from the turn of the century that my mother used to read to me just before bedtime. "Little Willie" rhymes were always my favorite. I used to recite them in Sunday School to the delight of my classmates and the horror of my teachers. I don't know why the poem suddenly wormed its way out of my subconscious and into my frontal lobe, but there it was along with a new one.

Little Willie, in the choir
Stole some wine, results were dire
He really dug the wine that killed 'im
And now we're digging Little William.

OK, technically the wine didn't kill him, but it was still a good "Little Willie" rhyme. However, I didn't share it with Nancy, who seemed to be having a hard time.

The vault was lifted out and set next to the pile of dirt, just beside the headstone that St. Barnabas had paid for. Bill unhooked the straps from the bucket, released the hammers that held the floor of the vault in place, and then reattached the straps to the handles on the top of the steel covering. The front-end loader slowly lifted the the vault clear of the coffin, leaving it resting on the ground, looking strangely out of place.

"It's much more difficult if a vault isn't used," Swallow explained, breaking his silence. "Or if it's an older burial. It can get fairly messy. We don't encourage the family to attend."

I nodded. "How do you open the coffin?"

"There's a crank that seals the coffin here on the end." Swallow produced a metal object from his pocket. "Not hard to get into when you know how. Bill will have it open shortly."

Nancy wasn't watching. She was looking off into the woods. I didn't blame her.

"That's it," said Bill, opening the lid and backing away.

Swallow and I leaned over the coffin. Willie looked much the same as I remembered him. I looked at him for a few moments and then realized that I hadn't taken a breath since the coffin had been opened, probably to protect my nose from the smell that I thought would hit me. I took a tentative breath. It was a musty odor, nothing more. Swallow reached in and took the cross from Willie's folded hands and, dangling it by the chain, handed it to me. I dropped it into a plastic bag.

"Is that all you need?"

"Yep. That's it. Make sure you wash your hands. The cross has poison on it."

"I always wash my hands," Swallow said.

Nancy and I didn't stay. We left the three men to reinter Willie without ceremony.

"Thanks for your help. Send your bill to the police department," I called over my shoulder as we got into my truck. I slipped the *German Requiem* into the CD player. Brahms was always good at a funeral. Nancy didn't say a word on the way to town.

I dropped Nancy off at the station with instructions to send Dave over to Boone that afternoon to deliver the cross to Kent Murphee. Then I headed over to the library for a church staff meeting that had been rescheduled due to the lack of electricity at St. Barnabas. Denise Franks, a member of the worship committee and a lay reader, worked at the St. Germaine library and often offered the little-used conference room for community meetings. I was fairly late, hoping that there hadn't been too much discussion. The services of Advent had been planned for months, but lately I didn't take anything for granted.

I got out of my Chevy and was walking up to the front door of the library when the entire group, minus Denise, trooped out. Herself was in the lead, still none too happy about her canceled conference. She walked right past me without a word. Beverly Greene was behind her followed by Georgia. They both stopped to chat and fill me in.

"She is mad," Georgia said.

"Well, at least she can't blame me."

"Yes she can," said Bev. "I don't know how exactly, but I get the distinct impression that it's all your fault."

"Next Wednesday night should be quite a show," Georgia added.

"What's happening next Wednesday?" I asked.

"Don't you know?" Georgia laughed. "It's a children's service. *The Christmas Crib.*"

I'm sure I had a look of dread on my face and Bev couldn't wait to fill me in.

"Mother Ryan is assigning parts this Sunday. The children are each supposed to be an animal visiting the manger. They have to write a song or a poem and sing it or recite it to the baby Jesus."

"You're not serious."

"Oh yes, she's serious," Georgia chimed in. "The parents have to make the costumes."

"You both are enjoying this way too much," I said.

"Oh, there's one other thing," Bev added with a sly smile. "The Bishop will be there."

On my way home, I stopped by the McCollough's trailer and dropped off some groceries. Moosey was munching away on the Butterfinger I had brought him when I had a brilliant idea. Or, conversely, a terrible idea. I didn't know which yet, but I knew I was committed. Or would be.

"Moosey, can you sing?"

"Oh, yes. I love to sing," he said through a mouth full of chocolate and forthwith determined to prove it. "Gladly the Cross-Eyed Bear—"

"That's good," I said laughing, trying to shut him up before he spewed half-chewed candy across the carpet. "That's one of my favorites. But I need you to learn a new song and sing it at a program next Wednesday night. Can you do it?"

"Can I, Ma?" Moosey asked, looking at Ardine, who was putting away the groceries.

"How late will it be?" she asked me. "He can't stay up too late."

"He'll be home by seven," I assured her. "You can come and watch."

"I have to work late at the tree farm till Christmas," Ardine said. "It's the busy season."

"OK. I'll bring the song by and we'll practice it. Then I'll pick him up on Wednesday and bring him home." I turned my attention back to Moosey who was licking the remaining chocolate off his fingers. "Can you memorize the song?"

"Sure I can! Listen! Je-sus loves the lid-dle chil-ren," he sang at the top of his lungs.

"Great," I said, quieting him down. "I'll bring you your song tomorrow. It's about a penguin."

"Je-sus loves the lid-dle pen-guins," Moosey sang as he ran out of the front door and down the steps. "All the pen-guins in the world!"

I said hello to Bud, who was reading the current *Wine Digest* in his room, and got his recommendation for a nice light dessert wine. I also checked in with Pauli Girl, who was doing a science report on deep sea fish, and then took my leave.

Now I needed a song and penguin costume.

I drove up to the house listening to the Christmas portion of *Messiah* and as I turned off the truck, I heard the phone ringing inside. I unlocked the door, went in and picked up the phone. On the other end of the transatlantic call was Geoffrey Chester, calling from jolly old England. Geoffrey was an accomplished composer and a headmaster at a choir school. He also was quite a linguist and lexicographer. I had put in a call to him a couple of days ago, but he'd been out of town.

"Here's the clue," I said after filling him in on the particulars and engaging in the appropriate amount of chit-chat.

> *I saw who did it. It's Him. It's Matthew.*
> *O hark the herald angels sing;*
> *The boy's descent which lifted up the world.*

"Ah," said Geoffrey, in his upper-class English accent. "It's obvious, of course."

It wasn't, and I could hear him scribbling away with a pen. I gave him a couple of minutes as he worked through the puzzle.

"The first line is a clue, but it's not central to the meaning. The second two lines are crucial. 'O hark the herald angels sing; the boy's descent which lifted up the world' appears to me to be an anagram. The syntax and word structure is such that an anagram would be the most obvious solution. From everything you've told me, the first line I would take to mean a hymn and the gospel of Matthew."

"That's what we thought, too. But we missed the anagram," I said. "I'll get someone working on it tonight."

"Let me know if you need me to come across and direct the investigation," Geoffrey said. "I'd enjoy some detective work for a change. These little blighters are driving me crazy."

I knew he was kidding about that last remark. The English hardly ever say "little blighters." I hung up the phone, walked into the kitchen to get some supper and looked out the kitchen window. The owl was back.

Chapter 12

Suddenly a shot rang out, the door flew open and there stood Amber Dawn, Personal Trainer.

"Amber," I said. "How nice to see you again. But you didn't have to shoot the lock off the door. It was open."

She hoisted her two thirty-eights back into her spandex where they belonged and sauntered into the office.

"Hi Denver. Isabel here yet?" she asked, ignoring me and dropping into a chair like a hundred and twenty pounds of beautiful cement.

"She's on her way up," Denver said, twirling the shotgun in her pudgy little hand like the head majorette in the homecoming parade. "She'll be here in a couple of minutes."

"How are you, Amber?" I was trying to get a friendly conversation started. I didn't like the way this day was turning out and Amber wasn't taking the bait. She did, however, reach out and take half of my sandwich. For a personal trainer, Amber Dawn ate like a racehorse.

Denver's eyes flashed toward the door and I knew that Isabel had arrived. I could have smelled her coming—wisteria, gin and cheap cigars, my favorite combination.

I looked up and there she was, six-feet-five-inches of hard right angles. She wore two shades of red that she had obviously selected to match her eyes. Her dark red hair hung to her shoulders in long, damp tendrils, gently swaying in the faint breeze of the ceiling fan like the legs of a couple of Spanish spiders doing the Tango D'Amore beneath her hat.

"Now that we're all here," growled Isabel, standing in the doorway, "we can get down to business."

"That's it?" said Meg, incredulously. "The 'Tango D'Amore?' Well, at least you have them all in the same room."

The next morning, before I left for town, I put a freshly deceased mouse on the window sill. I didn't want my little friend to go hungry and, truth be told, I liked to see him perching there. If I could entice him to come around now and then, all the better. One thing I wasn't short of, living in the woods, was mice. I cleaned out the mousetraps in the barn every morning and tossed the tiny corpses off the back deck for the wildlife. I didn't catch too many—two or three a week in the summer, more in the winter, but I decided to save them in the freezer. Even though I had written on the top of the coffee can in big letters "DEAD MICE," I made a mental note to tell Meg about it. Otherwise, I'd be picking up frozen rodents all over the kitchen. I also decided keep a couple of thawed ones in the vegetable crisper in a baggie. They'd make for easier digestion. I knew I'd better mention that to Meg as well.

I had recorded a cassette tape of Moosey's newly-composed song so he could learn it quickly. It was my experience that kids could learn anything if you put it on a tape and let them hear it a couple of times. And Moosey was smart. He might not know what was going on, but he'd be great as "The Penguin of Bethlehem." On my way into work, I dropped off a brand new boom box with the tape already loaded on the McCollough's front porch along with the words to the song and a note explaining what Moosey's part was in this program. The note also informed Ardine that the CD player was Moosey's reward for such hard and diligent work, thus insuring that Ardine would drill the song into Moosey's head until he had it cold. A pretty good deal, I thought. A singer *and* a teacher, all for $29.95 at Wal-Mart.

I was going to stop by Meg's house for some breakfast. Her mother was cooking waffles and once I got wind of it, I went fishing for an invitation like an angler on the first day of trout season.

"I can't meet you for coffee," Meg said when I called her earlier.

"Mother's making breakfast for me."

"Hmmm. What's she fixing?" I asked, beginning my finagle.

"Oh, just waffles and scrambled eggs. And maybe some country ham."

"Oh, well..."

"She has some blackberries to go on the waffles. You know, to go with that fresh hand-whipped cream and hot maple syrup."

I tried to sound very hungry by smacking my lips. "Well, I'll probably just try to get a stale bagel over at the gas station. It's going to be a busy day. I'd meet you for lunch, but I don't think I'll even have time to eat," I sighed.

"Oops, I've got to get the biscuits out of the oven or they won't taste very good with this homemade gravy. And stop drooling into the phone. You're invited."

"I'll be right over. One stop."

"Pick up some coffee 'cause we're out. See you in a bit."

"Two stops then. Bye."

I picked up a bag of coffee at The Slab but declined Pete's invitation for breakfast. I nodded "hello" to Rhiza and Malcolm, who were breakfasting at the corner table, before scooting out the door.

"Sorry, I have another date," I said, getting out the door quickly.

"See you later," I yelled as the door closed behind me.

The breakfast was every bit as good as I anticipated. Megan's mother, Ruby, was an excellent cook and I suspected that Meg was helping out as well. As a culinary tag-team, they couldn't be beat.

"Dee-licious," I said, settling back in my chair and wishing I had had the good sense to wear sweat-pants—or at least some old-man jeans with an elastic waist band. "You two are pretty good at word games. I need some help."

"How would you know we're good at word games? You never play with us," said Ruby pointedly, starting the dishes.

"Well, that's because I *hate* word games," I said as Meg punched me in the leg under the table. "I'm no good at that stuff. But I need someone to figure out an anagram."

I had Ruby's interest now. Meg's, too.

"What anagram?" Meg asked.

"Our clue," I said. "Geoffrey called last night. He thinks it's an anagram and I'm betting he's right."

"Do you have it with you?" Ruby asked, leaving the dishes and coming over to the table.

"I do indeed," I replied, and pulled out a piece of paper from my breast pocket.

O hark the herald angels sing;
The boy's descent which lifted up the world.

"Where's the first line?" asked Meg. "The part about Matthew?"

"We don't think it's part of the anagram. It doesn't fit the pattern."

"Why don't we get the Scrabble game out and lay out the letters," said Ruby, getting up and going to the hall closet.

"My thought exactly."

We laid the tiles on the table, spelled out the clue and came up a few letters short.

"We're going to need five more h's," Meg said. "I'll cut up some paper."

"I've got to get over to the station. Let me know if you come up with anything."

"We'll work on it," muttered Ruby, already rearranging the letters on the table into various words. "Is there anything specific we should be looking for?"

"We think it's a clue to the murder. That's all I can tell you about it. Thanks for a lovely breakfast." I closed the front door behind me leaving the two women huddled over the table..

I arrived at the office about ten minutes later, just in time to hear Dave's end of the conversation on the phone.

"What do you mean, no parade? Listen, Marta, we've had it on the schedule all year. Kiwanis Club Christmas Parade, December eighteenth. No, you didn't do the parade last year. It was two years ago. Last year Kiwanis did the Living Crèche. Yes, I know it was well-received. Well," said Dave, wrapping up his futile conversation, "*you're* going to have to tell Pete."

"What's up?" I asked, knowing the answer was going to be bad news.

"The Kiwanis Club isn't going to sponsor the Christmas parade this year. *They* want to do the Living Crèche."

"Isn't it the Rotary's turn for the crèche."

"According to us and Bob Solomon it is. They've already built a new scene, arranged for all new costumes and hired Seymour Krebbs' camel."

"A camel. That's pretty good."

Dave went on, "Marta says that the Kiwanis Club got permission from the Rotary to do their crèche again because it was such a big hit last year. You know, with the petting zoo for the kids and the llamas and all."

"I never did understand how a South American animal made it all the way to Bethlehem."

"Probably on a boat. Anyway, Bob says he didn't agree to anything with Marta and it's the Kiwanis Club's turn to host the parade. Apparently, the Rotarians really spent a bundle to outdo the Kiwanians' crèche from last year."

"Sheesh. Does Pete know?" I asked, shaking my head and heading into my office.

"No. I told Marta to call him, but I don't think she will till it's too late to do anything about it. He'll have to hear it from you."

"It's already too late to do anything about it. Have there been any parade committee meetings?"

"Not that I'm aware of."

"Is anyone expecting to be in it? You know, bands, floats, stuff like that?"

Dave looked at his information from last year's parade and flipped through the papers. "Nope. They would have had to send in an entrance fee by November 10th. No one sent any information out, so no one sent in a fee."

"That's that, then. At least no one will be mad. Maybe it will all just disappear," I said. But I doubted it.

I called Pete and gave him the scoop on the parade. To paraphrase his immediate utterance, rendering it inoffensive to human ears and allowing it to float harmlessly into the stratosphere, knocking down a few birds that might be passing by, but generally doing no permanent damage: "We are not amused." Actually Pete is one of the only people I know that can say a thirteen-word sentence using nothing but expletives. It's an art really. He works in profanity the way another artist might work in watercolors, each word carrying various hues and subtleties not available to the casual curser. His work in the field of gerunds alone would make him a legend in any seaport on the east coast.

I held the phone away from my ear as Pete voiced his displeasure at the situation and took the opportunity to loudly emphasize a number of details concerning the Kiwanian's common ancestry and the moral character of all their sisters and mothers.

Later that afternoon, I dropped by the Farthing residence to see how mother and daughter were faring on the word games.

"Come on in. We've got a couple of things worked out," Meg said opening the door. Her dark hair was tousled and pulled back. She was wearing jeans and one of my old sweatshirts. She looked ravishing.

I went into the kitchen and saw the Scrabble tiles still spread across the table, words placed hither and yon, but with no discernible pattern that I could see.

"There's a lot of letters," said Ruby. "You could make almost anything out of them. Here's one for instance."

She wants to sing Bill Gaither tunes.
Choked chef hardly plowed the herd.

How's that?" Med added.

"Pretty bad," I said. "I like the part about the Bill Gaither tunes, though."

Meg was digging through her stack of papers. "Here's one."

Ring thanks. God real. He heals.
When rested, bathed, clothed, I putt softly.

I started looking through the papers on the table and read several anagrams that really meant nothing that I could see.

Bad newsletters deduct the filthy photo
Hello, earth-shaking gardens

This filthy snow troubles hat depth
detected large longer handshake

"Hmmm, interesting, but I don't recognize anything usable," I said. "What about this? We think that the first line. 'I saw who did it. It's him. It's Matthew,' is part of the clue and that Matthew is the gospel and 'it's him' refers to a hymn, right?" I asked the two ladies, now watching me intently and nodding in the affirmative.

"Then, that being the case," I continued, "maybe the anagram is a hymn title, which would narrow our search considerably."

"I'll get the hymnal," said Meg.

"And I'll pour the coffee," added Ruby, getting up and quickly returning with three mugs, which she placed on the table amongst the scattered Scrabble tiles. I always appreciated a coffee mug.

Meg returned with two copies of The Hymnal 1982, and I recognized the inscription on the front of each: "Property of St. Barnabas Church." She looked a little sheepish as she handed one to her mother.

"I'm just *borrowing* them. You aren't going to arrest me, are you?"

"Not today, my dear," I said sipping my coffee.

"We should probably start with the Christmas section," Ruby suggested. "The anagram seems pretty Christmasy to me. The first Christmas hymn is number 77. I think this will go pretty fast. Once we rule a hymn out, we can go on to the next one."

"Great idea," said Meg, opening her own book. "I'll take 78."

Thirty-eight minutes later, while rummaging around the refrigerator for sandwich fixin's, I heard Ruby cry out, "Bingo! I've got it!"

"That was quick," I said, munching on a dill pickle and pulling out some leftovers.

Meg looked over at Ruby's paper. "I was on 93, so it must be 94."

Ruby nodded and pointed to the anagram, then to her scribblings.

O hark the herald angels sing;
The boy's descent which lifted up the world.
While shepherds watched their flocks by night,
all seated on the ground.

"You have to admit it's good," I said.

Meg was already coming back into the room with a Bible.

"Let's see. Hymn 94. Matthew 9:4." She thumbed through the

pages quickly. "And Jesus, knowing their thoughts said, 'Why are you thinking evil in your hearts?'" She pondered the scripture for a moment. "Well, that doesn't help a bit, does it?"

"Hang on. Let's not despair. We know what the anagram means. We just have to figure out the rest of the clue." I was trying to be as hopeful as possible, but in reality, I had no idea what the verse had to do with the murder, if anything. We might be on the totally wrong track, but I didn't want to say as much after such hard work. So, I said the next best thing.

"Let's have a sandwich."

Chapter 13

"Now that we're all here," growled Isabel, standing in the doorway, "we can get down to business." Her voice was low, low as my Apple Computer stock options.

"You know what we want, don't 'cha?" Denver asked absently. She had put down the shotgun and her attention was focused on the three hymnals she was deftly juggling. She was good. I had to admit it.

Yes, I knew what they wanted. Denver Tweed, Amber Dawn and Isabel Gerhardt. Separately, three gals you wouldn't mind seeing dancing the Lambada in your neighbor's Sunday school class. Together, they formed the Emmaus Gang—and were three of the most wanted women in the history of the Episcopate. They needed the goods on the Bishop. Blackmail was their only prospect to make it off of his Ten Most Wanted List, and I had just what they wanted.

"You might as well just give it to us and we'll be on our way," said Isabel, taking a cigar from off my desk and lighting it up.

"I doubt it. You'll have to kill me. Otherwise you'd be afraid that I'd squeal like last year's Easter entree." I lit another stogie myself, matching her puff for puff.

"We don't have to kill him, do we?" chirped Amber in alarm. "I really kinda like him." She lit a cigar too, her peepers blinking like baby blue Christmas tree lights.

Isabel sneered. "Like a gold ring in a pig's snout is a beautiful woman without good sense."

"What?" squeaked Amber confusedly, but thrusting out her chest like the photo-finish of a zeppelin race at the prospect of being called "beautiful" by anyone.

"Proverbs 11:22," quoted Isabel smugly as Denver lit up the last cigar in the box, making the atmosphere in my office the ecological equivalent of Los Angeles in June.

"I was just wondering, Isabel," I said, trying to draw her into a theological discussion. "Does the pig snout refer to a literal pig snout, or is the author taking a metaphoric view and using the pig snout to represent the unclean noses of all the heathen races?"

"Don't start with me," Isabel grunted. "Just give me the papers we want and we'll be on our way."

I didn't believe her for a second.

I had a couple of calls to make. The first was to the Norcostco Costume Company in Atlanta. I had them send a penguin costume to St. Barnabas and charge it to the rector's discretionary account. I didn't have Moosey's exact size, but I was pretty sure I was close. The second was to Pete Moss.

"Hi Pete. Did you get the crèche situation straightened out?"

"Nope. These idiots both want to put up a living nativity and there's no stopping them. The Rotary Club has the lot on Main and 13th on the south side. The Kiwanis Club is a block down on the north side. It's going to be a zoo. Literally."

"Maybe," I contemplated, "but just maybe there's room in this crazy, mixed-up world for two nativity scenes. Why can't we all just get along?"

"Shut up, Hayden."

I picked Moosey up at school on Tuesday and took him by the church to practice the penguin song. Late afternoons were perfect for rehearsing and it's the time when I get all my practicing done. The church was generally deserted and today was no exception. I thought it might be a little spooky for someone who wasn't used to a great silent church, but Moosey walked down the aisle, stood proudly on the steps of the nave and sang through his song with organ accompaniment just like a champ, never missing a word.

"Moosey, that was great!" I yelled down to him from the choir loft as he was taking the bow we had practiced.

"Can we do it again?" he called back, the thrill of performance still in his eager face.

"You bet. But once more should probably do it."

We went through it a second time, which is two times more than Herself ever rehearsed anything. When the song was finished, Moosey took his bow and came racing up the stairs to the choir loft.

"Your costume will be here tomorrow," I told him, as I shut down the beast.

"Is it a good costume?"

"The best penguin costume they had."

"Momma doesn't think I should be sangin' this song in church, ya know," Moosey said, happily munching on a Zagnut bar I had slipped him as a reward.

"It'll be fine. You're doing a great job."

"I like to sing, all right. I shore do."

Before taking Moosey home for the evening, I stopped by the church office to deliver the hymn numbers for Sunday. Moosey was finishing up his candy bar just as Mother Ryan's door opened and Rhiza Walker exited her office, closing the door behind her. It didn't take a detective to tell she had been crying.

"Oh, hello, Hayden," she sniffed, rather formally I thought, as she dabbed at her nose with a tissue.

"Hi, Rhiza. You OK?"

"I guess. I have to go."

Her lilting squeak was gone, replaced by a sadder, older timbre. She was out the office door before I could say anything else. I hoped there wasn't anything wrong between her and Malcolm. I liked them both.

I had gotten used to seeing the owl sitting on the window sill each night as I returned from town so I was disappointed when I pulled up and my headlights failed to pick up his yellow eyes glowing in the dark. I went inside and dropped a CD of Charpentier's *Midnight Mass for Christmas* on the Wave and got a San Miguel Dark out of the beer fridge. It was a Filipino beer, dark and rich and just right, I thought, for drinking while listening to music of the French Baroque and fixing a quick supper. Maybe I was just being a beer snob, but I liked to think of it as getting into the Christmas spirit.

I opened the window, lifted the screen and was getting the baggie of thawed mouse carcasses out of the refrigerator when, without a sound, the owl appeared at the window. As I watched, not moving, he stepped across the sill just as nicely as you please, shaking his white feathers as if tossing off the dampness of the evening and with his head moving independently of his body, took in the whole of the kitchen decor. Not knowing what else to do, as the creature tentatively strolled the counter, and not wanting to scare him into flying into the interior of the cabin, I opened the baggie and held out an ex-mouse, dangling it by its tail. I moved slowly forward but the owl didn't react until I was within an arm's reach. Then he tilted his head about 45 degrees, opened his beak and took the mouse out of my hand. He hopped back onto the sill, the mouse still in his beak and leaped without a sound into the night. I closed the window behind him, wondering if this was going to be a nightly event or if he just liked the French Baroque.

The Wednesday evening service was in the bulletin as "The Christmas Crib." I had, graciously I thought, volunteered to play the prelude, the postlude and congregational hymn. Also in the bulletin were the names of the participants. Herself was the narrator. There were two silent roles—Mary and Joseph—played by

Gerry and Wilma Fleming, a new young couple in the church, a non-silent screaming baby Jesus role played by the Fleming's five-month-old baby girl, and a total of six children, including Moosey, portraying the animals coming to the manger. I had made sure that Moosey was last on the program and also that Meg was there to help him with his costume and entrance.

I started off with an improvisation on *Joy to the World* and, as I finished up, was surprised to look down and see the church almost full. Mother Ryan must have done some advertising.

"We welcome you this evening to the manger at Bethlehem," she began after she took her place at the lectern. "This is a new idea of mine to incorporate the children of St. Barnabas into our Christmas celebration."

I snarled. We'd been doing this for years, but we called it the Christmas Pageant.

"And now let us journey to the manger and join with the children as they offer up their songs and poems to the holy child."

The Flemings had taken their places, kneeling and wedging themselves inside the brown refrigerator carton stable before putting their baby into the newly constructed manger which, I hoped, was strong enough to hold a mad, wiggling twenty pounder. I had begun to play the first hymn, *Away In A Manger*, when baby Jesus let out his first wail.

Away in a manger, no crib for a bed,
The little Lord Jesus lay down his sweet head.
The stars in the bright sky looked down where he lay,
The little Lord Jesus asleep in the hay.

Each line of the hymn was punctuated by several solos from the baby section of the Holy Family Choir. Bev and Georgia were sitting up in the choir loft balcony, in their usual front-row seats, leaning over the rail and watching the festivities.

"I thought the baby Jesus was *asleep* in the hay," Georgia quipped.

"Wait till they get to the part about 'no crying he makes,'" said Beverly.

We finished the hymn, and not exactly quietly. Everyone, including me, was trying to drown out the sound of Baby Jesus' vocalizations which, by this time, were stentorian in nature. The performance may have been the most robust version of *Away In A Manger* that has ever been my pleasure to accompany. By the last stanza, I was using the full organ, including trumpets and 32' reeds, the wailing baby matching me decibel for decibel. Herself was beginning to seethe.

At the triumphant finish of the hymn, she was glaring up at me as if this complication was my fault, or at least something that I had control over. I shrugged at her in a very obvious, theatrical fashion, hoping that she would understand that this problem was not *my* fault and the fiasco thus far was totally on her shoulders. Thus far.

She walked over to Wilma and said something to her quietly. Previously looking as if she wanted to fall through the floor with embarrassment, Wilma now raised her head defiantly, picked up her screaming child wrapped in swaddling clothes, marched down the center aisle and out the front door, leaving her husband looking confused and not quite sure of his loyalties. Was he to follow his wife and baby out of the church or stay true to his theatrical character and play the role out to the bitter end? He stayed. I suspected that he would find out he had made the wrong choice when he got home.

Mother Ryan had never been known for her tact and I'm quite sure she had insulted both mother and child. When she suggested that Wilma take up her child and go, she probably meant for her to use the side exit, but it was not to be. You can't insult a woman's baby and then expect her to leave by the side door. And since she was leaving by the front door, I decided to "play her out" with a rousing number. The evening was shaping up splendidly.

Since Joseph, sans Mary, was still stuck in the refrigerator box with an empty manger, Mother Ryan walked into the congregation, pulled a teenaged girl from the front pew and led her up to the steps. The girl was confused at first, letting herself be led like a lamb to the slaughter, but then, realizing what the rector had in mind, pulled away, and went racing back, choosing the safety of her anonymous pew to the sure humiliation of nativic thespianism. All this to *Bring A Torch, Jeannette Isabella* set in a wonderful carnival-like toccata and improvised beautifully by *moi*. I hadn't spent one entire summer of grad school as a theater organist in Minneapolis for nothing.

Mother Ryan, now short two Marys and one baby, went back to the lectern as I finished up the final grandiose chords.

"Holy smokes," whispered Bev. "She's mad."

"I can see her jaw twitching from up *here*," agreed Georgia, still whispering.

Everyone in the audience became very still and a deathly hush fell over the congregation as Herself reached for her sheaf of papers. Joseph had decided it would be best for him to make an unobtrusive exit, but she saw him move and whipped around, pointing a long bony finger in his direction. He froze, eyes wide. Turning back to the lectern, Mother Ryan began her narration in low, measured tones that were unlike anything I've ever heard.

"When Jesus was born in Bethlehem," she said in a low, flat voice devoid of all inflection and humanity, "the animals came to the manger to see the newborn Savior." She spit out the words as if they were poison, then looked up over her half-glasses, her cold eyes narrowing as she surveyed her prey, With a snarl on her lips, she bared her teeth and dared anyone to make a sound. No one moved. No sound was made. The tiger had stepped forth into the forest and all living things were huddled in silent terror. I noticed Bishop Douglas in the third row. He was beginning to squirm uncomfortably.

This last line by Herself was obviously the cue for the first animal to arrive. In, from the back of the church, came what

153

appeared to be a very frightened sheep wearing a cute little costume made of a fluffy wool-like substance. His mother had begun by urging him forward down the aisle, but it had become apparent that this sheep was no fool and he wasn't going down to face the tiger without his mommy. His mother looked up at me in desperation and I motioned for her to accompany her little lamb up to the front. While they walked to the front, I played a chorus of the *Echo Carol* to break the tension. The sheep stood in front of the congregation by the cardboard stable.

"What do you have to say to the Baby Jesus?" hissed the rector, obviously now playing the well-known part of the Antichrist of Bethlehem.

"I am the little sheep. I wander day and night," the sheep said in a quivering voice, still clutching his mother's hand.

"I've come to see the stable," he paused, thinking.

"A great and glorious sight," his mother whispered to him.

"A great and glorious sight," the sheep bleated, now close to panic.

"Good job," his mother whispered and led him to an empty pew that was reserved for the animals.

I expected some applause but there was none. Not a creature was stirring.

There was no introduction from Mother Ryan for the second animal. A donkey. I played him in with *The Friendly Beasts*. He was an older child. Third grade I would guess.

"I am the donkey, shaggy and brown," he sang in a quavering soprano.

"I carried the maid, uphill and down."

He looked over at Herself and his blood ran cold. I suspect that children can sense evil much like animals can. If there was more to his song, we never heard it. He finished abruptly and moved to the pew.

The cat never made it to the front. She was halfway down the aisle before screaming and bolting for the front door. It's too bad too because I had just started playing "Alley Cat" to lighten the mood a little. I stopped halfway through a phrase, letting my fingers drag along the keys for effect.

Georgia had been watching the proceedings from the stairwell. With a view of both the church and the narthex, she could cue me in on which animals were coming up so I could be prepared. Suddenly she stood up and in a loud stage whisper that I'm afraid, in that deathly quiet, everyone could hear, said "That's it, Hayden. They've all left except Moosey."

"Is he ready?" I asked.

"Oh yes. He's ready."

I looked up at Herself. She was the Ancient Gargoyle of Christmas, still holding the congregation in her Medusa-like thrall from which no one dared escape.

Then Moosey made his entrance.

He came down the aisle in his penguin costume. It was black with a white front, two flippers where his arms were, orange high-top tennis shoes, a black hood topped by a red stocking cap and his nose was painted orange. I had vetoed the beak that came with the costume. I wanted everyone to see his face. He waddled down the aisle just as we had rehearsed and took his place on the top step right in front of the stable. I didn't give him any traveling music. He was on his own.

He stood there for a moment, perfectly serious, then he pointed a flipper up to the choir loft and said in a loud voice, the way we had rehearsed it, "Maestro, if you please!"

I played him the introduction and he began to sing in his loudest soprano voice.

There ain't no ice in Bethlehem,
I traveled here you see,
To greet the Baby Jesus,
But it's too dang hot fer me.

It was an original tune and we had put in a little dance between verses. The stifled laughter from the congregation was now beginning to erupt like the first puffs of ignition from a long-neglected engine. By the time Moosey got to the chorus the engine was at full throttle.

Oh them floes, them icy floes!
To see them once again is my goal.
Oh them floes, them icy floes!
Just take me back to the South Pole.

My feathers all are matted now,
My beak is almost thawed,
It sure is one big price to pay,
To greet the little Lord.

More laughter, as Moosey two-stepped clumsily across the stage, his flippers slapping together in time.

Oh them floes, them icy floes!
To see them once again is my goal.

People were beginning to clap now and sing along with the chorus, ignoring the glaring rector and enjoying themselves immensely.

Oh them floes, them icy floes!
Just take me back to the South Pole.

Moosey headed into the last verses to hushes from the audience so everyone could hear him, although he was singing at the top of his lungs. He was hamming it up now, Gilbert and Sullivan style, three-feet-six-inches of lovable penguin strutting across the podium, his orange high-tops slapping against the oak floor with every step he took.

I'm whaling 'cause I'm hungry,
And there ain't no fish to find.
I'm eeling very sharkish,
Squid this salmon on my mind;

I flounder 'cause I'm crabby,
There's no oysters in this house.
I'll give my sole to Jesus,
'Cause my bass is headin' south.

The hoots and cheers that went up from the congregation at that moment drowned out the beginning of Moosey's last chorus. They rushed the podium, knocked over the refrigerator box, lifted Moosey to their shoulders and carried him, singing, en masse, out the front door and into the street as I improvised a couple of choruses on the organ, playing with all the gusto I could muster. As I played the final chord, I looked up to the front. Joseph was the only one left, silently looking over the ruins of his cardboard stable. Mother Ryan and the bishop were nowhere to be seen. I looked over at Georgia, Beverly and now Meg, who had joined us after Moosey had made his entrance. They were at the balcony rail, holding hands. Tears of joy were running down their faces.

"Now *that's* preaching," Georgia said.

Chapter 14

Question: What's the difference between a soprano and a terrorist? Answer: You can negotiate with a terrorist. Isabel Gerhardt wasn't taking "no" for an answer.

Question: What's the difference between an alto and a piranha? Answer: Lipstick. Denver Tweed was 225 pounds of pit bull looking for a poodle fight. I wasn't sure I could take her if the playing field was level. And it wasn't.

Question: What did the Bishop's Personal Trainer get on her SATs? Answer: Fingernail polish. Although she had been a music major, Amber Dawn didn't know much about music. She thought that a sackbut was a choral singer over forty. Still, she was smart enough to land on her feet more often than on her back. At least that's what she wanted me to believe.

Question: What's the ideal weight for a bishop? Answer: About two-and-a-half pounds, including the urn. The Bishop had gotten me into this mess and he wasn't getting off scott free. Sure, he was my employer, but if the only way out of this was to give him up, well, so be it. There were other jobs in this city.

I reached for a book on the upper shelf.

"Watch it, handsome," said Amber, pulling out one of her 38's and leveling it at yours truly. "Take it slow and easy."

"You won't believe this," I told Meg as we stood in the kitchen, facing the open window, each holding a dead mouse. Meg had hers at arms length with a look of disgust on her face as the strains of Hugo Distler's *Christmas Story* filled the house.

"It's a great piece, don't you think?" I asked her, listening to the music and gently conducting with my rodent-baton. "It puts me in the Christmas spirit. I'm reminded of a poem."

"I hope it's the one where 'not a creature was stirring, not even this dead mouse,'" she quipped. "So far, this makes my list of 'ten worst dates.'"

"How can you possibly say that, standing here in a freezing house, listening to Hugo Distler and dangling a dead mouse by the tail?"

"Gee. I wonder," she said, shrugging. "This one is slightly worse than my blind date with the four-foot Mexican named Bernardo who didn't speak any English. As I recall, I ended up in the back seat of the car teaching him to play tic-tac-toe on the steamed-up windows while my roommate made out with her boyfriend in the front seat."

"And this one is worse?" I asked, somewhat suspiciously.

"Well, at least there weren't any dead mice involved."

About two minutes later, with a flash of feathers, the owl appeared on the sill and stepped through the window into the kitchen as if he'd been doing it all his life. I held my mouse out to him first and he took it gently in his beak. Then, as the owl looked expectantly at Meg, she gingerly held out her suspended offering. With his beak full, he balanced on one leg and lifted a talon to take the snack from Meg's hand. With two mice securely in his possession, he took a little leap to get himself airborne, then disappeared through the open window and into the night.

We just stood there for a few moments, staring out after the wild creature. Meg was stunned into silence. But not for long.

"That was great!" she whispered. "Will he come back?"

"We can't leave the window open all night. It's freezing out there. Anyway, he doesn't usually come back. Not till tomorrow night, around six."

"OK," she said. "This has moved way up on the date list. What are you going to name him?"

"Name him?"

"He has to have a name. How 'bout...Blinky?"

"Blinky?" I'm sure my loathing was apparent.

"Hooty?"

"What kind of name is Hooty? I might as well name him Owly. Or Mr. Peepers."

"Yes, Mr. Peepers."

"No!" I almost shouted, closing the window. "Not Mr. Peepers!"

"Take it easy," said Megan, laughing. "I was just kidding. How about that owl in *The Once and Future King*?"

"Archimedes."

"Yes, that's it. Archimedes. Will that do?"

"Well, it's certainly better than Mr. Blinky."

"You mean Mr. Peepers," she corrected.

"Archimedes it is," I said, knowing when to cut my losses. "Archimedes the Owl."

We had a breakfast meeting at The Slab. I walked into the restaurant at about 8:30. I didn't see Pete, but thought he might be in the back cooking. Dave and Nancy had already started. Breakfast, that is, not the meeting.

"What're you having?" I asked, pulling out my chair, putting my iBook on the table and taking a seat.

"Pahcahds," mumbled Dave unintelligibly, munching happily, syrup hanging heavily on his chin.

"If I was a detective, I'd deduce that you were having 'pancakes,' but it's hard to tell," I said and handed him a napkin.

Nancy was having the breakfast special. Country ham, eggs, grits, and biscuits with gravy.

"How do you keep your schoolgirl figure?"

She looked at me over a forkful of eggs mixed with grits. "I work out five days a week. What's your secret?"

"Never mind," I said, changing the subject before the meeting turned ugly. Of the three of us, I was definitely *not* the one to be casting aspersions in regard to girth.

"I like your computer, Boss. Is it a new one?"

Dave had finished up his bite of pancakes and was doing his best to clean up his chin.

"Pretty new."

I fired it up as I gave Doris my order. I had put my "list" on the computer. It was easier to change it on the word processor and I was changing it pretty often.

"Did we hear from the lab?" I asked Nancy.

"I have it right here." She shuffled through the papers that she had stacked beside her plate. "Here we go."

She scanned the report quickly to refresh her memory and then gave us the highlights.

"The cross was saturated with oleandrin, nerin, digitoxigenin, and rosagenin." She hesitated slightly over the unfamiliar names, but read them off without a noticeable error, then checked them again to make sure she had read them correctly before continuing. "The same chemicals that were found in Willie Boyd's system. Kent Murphee says that the cross was probably boiled in the pot with the oleander because the olive wood absorbed a huge amount of the toxins. And because it was boiled down, it was much more potent than the oleander itself."

"We thought as much," I said, holding my coffee cup up for Doris to fill. I opened the file on the iBook. "Let's see what we have."

"Well, at least the computer is a step up from your little list," said Nancy.

When?

Willie Boyd was killed on Friday afternoon at approximately 5:12 p.m. Beverly Green saw him at 5:10 making a phone call to the police. He stole Loraine Ryan's olive-wood cross from the sacristy and, according to Bev, kissed it before going up to the choir loft where he had a drink, threw up on the organ and died. Willie had stolen three cases of wine earlier that afternoon, hidden them in the trunk of his car and drank from one of the bottles that he had hidden in the choir loft. The wine wasn't poisoned, but the cross was.

Who?

We still don't know, but we had the clue figured out. Sort of.

I saw who did it. It's Him. It's Matthew.
O hark the herald angels sing;
The boy's descent which lifted up the world.

The clue is an anagram. We think that the first line refers to a hymn number and the Gospel of Matthew. The second two lines are an anagram for

While shepherds watched their flocks by night, all seated on the ground.

While shepherds watched is hymn number 94. Matthew 9:4 says, "Why are you thinking evil in your hearts?" No help there. Not yet.

Mother Ryan wasn't off the hook. She knew something, of that I was sure. She was in the kitchen and knew about the oleander broth.

Why?

I'm pretty sure that Willie's death was an accident. It was a murder, all right, but I suspect that the object of the murder wasn't Willie at all, but Loraine Ryan. There wasn't any way that the murderer could possibly know that Willie, infatuation or not, would steal Mother Ryan's cross and kiss it. Herself, on the other hand, would kiss the cross as a matter of ritual whenever she put it on. Eventually, she would get a fatal dose of the poison. So who would want Mother Ryan dead? Other than everyone in the parish, I mean?

How?

Oleander poisoning. The chemicals were absorbed though Willie Boyd's oral membranes. The olive-wood cross from the Holy Land was the murder weapon.

My breakfast arrived just as we got to "What."

Don't forget 'What?', Nancy smirked. "What?"

"Ham and eggs," I said. " With a side of hash browns."

St. Germaine was a picture postcard in the month of December. There were tiny white lights covering every fence, lightpost and storefront in the downtown area. Cars were discreetly parked and all the shopkeepers had decorated their establishments with wreaths and greenery making Main Street look like Martha Stewart was spending the holidays. With the first snowfall, the effect would be breathtaking.

The Rotary Club was building their Christmas crèche on the south side of Main Street. The Kiwanis Club was putting theirs up on the north side, one block down. It was hard to tell, at this juncture, which club would have the larger display. The Rotarians had a couple of crews at work courtesy of Hatteberg's Construction. The electricians were finishing up in the stable area, installing the electric "flickering torches" and indirect "holy aura" lighting around the manger, and the carpenters were hard at work on the second story of the inn. The balcony for the innkeeper's wife to stand on and wave to the visitors of the Holy Family was shaping up nicely but was being reinforced by extra timbers. Apparently the role of the innkeeper's wife was going again to Mrs. Horst, a woman of healthy Wagnerian proportions.

The Kiwanians were working on more of a barn idea, choosing not to include the inn in their depiction of the Nativity. They had hired four Amish builders to put their barn up, figuring, rightfully so, that they'd do a great job. It would be a real shame to tear it down after Christmas. Their barn was a 3/4 size post and beam, and included a hayloft where the angels would be stationed, singing their praises to the Holy Child. The Kiwanians also planned to include a petting zoo for the smaller children along with the standard cow, lamb and miniature donkey. The Rotarians had the camel—a definite crowd pleaser. It was shaping up to be quite a contest.

I was in the church office picking out the hymns for Christmas Eve. Meg and I were on our way to the Christmas Concert at Appalachian State and she was, as usual, there to offer her suggestions.

"How about this," I said to Marilyn, who was in charge of typing the bulletin. "*O Come All Ye Faithful, Hark! The Herald Angels Sing, O Little Town of Bethlehem,* and *Silent Night.*"

"What about *Lo, How A Rose?*" asked Meg, flipping through the hymnal.

"We're singing that one on the third Sunday of Advent."

"How about *Joy To The World ?*"

"Christmas morning."

"Well, they sound pretty good to me," agreed Meg, closing the hymnal, obviously anxious to get to the concert. She usually put up more of an argument.

Marilyn was typing the hymns into the bulletin template looking up the hymn numbers as she went.

"Which version of *O Little Town of Bethlehem*?" she asked.

"The second one. *St. Louis.*"

Meg and I looked at each other and both of us had the same thought at the same time. She grabbed the hymnal that she had put back on the shelf and turned quickly to Hymn 94, *While Shepherds Watched Their Flocks By Night.*

"Sure enough," said Meg. "We didn't look far enough. Hymn 95. Same text, different tune. Where's a Bible?"

"What's going on?" asked Marilyn.

"Meg's just trying to solve the murder."

"Really? That's great! Who did it?"

"We'll know momentarily," I said, finding a Bible on the shelf and handing to Meg.

At that moment Herself's door banged open and she stepped out into the church office. I had no doubt that she had heard us through the door. She didn't say a word, but most of the remaining color had drained from her already deathly pallor, leaving the rouge on her cheeks and her bright red lipstick standing out like clown makeup.

Meg didn't notice her, or if she did, didn't pay her any mind and read aloud from Matthew 9:5. "For which is easier, to say 'your sins are forgiven,' or to say 'Rise, and walk?'"

Mother Ryan glared at me with a look of unbridled hate, turned on her heel and went right back into her office, closing the door firmly behind her. We all noticed that her phone extension button on Marilyn's console lit up almost immediately.

"Holy Cow," I muttered. "We really rang *her* bell."

"I don't believe it," said Meg, reading the passage again, this time to herself.

"What?" asked Marilyn. "Who did it?"

"It might be misleading," offered Meg. "The real murderer could be someone else."

"Yes, it could," I agreed.

"Who?" asked Marilyn. "C'mon. Who was it?"

Meg looked at me for permission to tell her. I just shrugged and Meg felt free to spill the beans.

"The clue might be deceptive," Meg slowly repeated to Marilyn as if she were telling a child, making sure that Marilyn understood. "It could be someone else."

"Yes, yes. I *get* it. It could be someone else," said Marilyn with exasperation, still waiting for the final shoe to drop.

"And you can't tell anyone," I admonished.

"I know!" Marilyn dropped into her chair, exhausted by the effort of trying to get information from either of us.

Finally Megan had pity on her.

"Rhiza. It was Rhiza Walker."

Chapter 15

I weighed my choices like a butcher on Good Friday and decided to give up the Bishop. If I played my cards right, he might never know it was me that dealt him the inside straight.

"Easy now," I said to Amber who was leveling her gun directly at yours truly. "I'm just getting the photos you want."

"We'll need the financial records, too," said Isabel, now beginning to gloat.

"You want the whole thing, or just the interesting parts?"

"We want it all," Amber squeaked. "Everything you've got."

I pulled down the file from behind the book where I had stashed it against the Bishop's employment whims. I looked on it as my retirement plan, but it was disappearing as fast as cheese snacks at an Oprah Winfrey book signing.

"What're you going to do with this?" I asked Isabel, who was obviously the ringleader of the trio. I put the file on the desk.

"We won't use it unless we have to. The Bishop has got to back off of our Scratch-N-Sniff Anthems."

"I think you're lying. The anthems have nothing to do with this."

I wasn't buying the Scratch-N-Sniff ploy. It stank like wet dog aftershave. I've suspected for a while that Isabel was after the Bishop's job. It was conceivable that she could get elected if she could disgrace the Bishop, force him to resign and get someone to put her name in the hat during the convocation. She had the votes or she had the goods on almost everyone. But I didn't know how she'd pull it off and I still had to get out of my immediate predicament.

"Isabel," I asked innocently. "If you become Bishop, will you still need an liturgy Detective?"

"How did he know?" asked Amber Dawn, Personal Trainer.

"Shut up Amber," said Isabel. "He doesn't know anything."

"He does now," said Denver, taking off her tweed jacket and showing off biceps as big as canned hams. She cracked her knuckles and started walking towards me.

I saw it now. Isabel Gerhardt as Bishop, Amber Dawn, her Personal Trainer and Denver Tweed as the muscle.

And the muscle was coming after me.

"Things are starting to pick up," said Megan. "But what on earth does that mean? 'Like a butcher on Good Friday?' And if you dealt the Bishop an inside straight, he'd be pleased, wouldn't he? Still, I sense the semblance of a plot."

"Don't be so sure. I've been known to fake a story line quicker than a Connie Chung news crew just to get in some bad similes and a metaphor or two."

"But, darling," Meg said, her tongue planted firmly in her cheek, "that would just be *wrong.* Think of the poor children out there that might stumble upon this story and read it accidentally. They could be permanently scarred and you would be held educationally accountable."

"The story is not to blame," I said, taking a sip of wine, "it's the reader. But I think you may be right. I should use my literary powers for good instead of evil."

"I agree. Not only that, but the mushrooms are ready."

What would come to be known locally as *The Crèche War* was shaping up nicely. The Kiwanians were all set to begin their show on Thursday evening and run it each night through Sunday. Four evenings, all beginning at 7:00 and going until 8:30. An hour-and-a-half outside in December was about all the shepherds could stand. Mary and Joseph could bundle up, the wise men would be layering, but the shepherds and the angels were out there in the wind and it was going to be very cold, long underwear or not. So the Kiwanians were set. That is, until they found out what the Rotarians were up to.

The Rotarians, knowing the Kiwanians' schedule, decided that they would begin on Thursday and go from 6:30 to 9:00. The Kiwanians, having none of that, decided that they would up the ante by adding another day and another half hour. Finally the town council stepped in and set the hours, citing the need for police protection and traffic control. It wasn't true, but it worked. The hours were set for both groups. Thursday through Saturday, 7:00 to 8:30.

I met with Nancy and Dave over a cup of coffee at The Slab. I missed our breakfast gathering due to oversleeping. Nancy and Dave had no problem eating breakfast without me and charging it to the department. I couldn't blame them.

We sipped our coffee and were on our third cup, finishing our old business and the upcoming Christmas plans before I told Nancy and Dave about the clue that Meg and I had discovered. Pete, walking by for the twelfth time with the coffee pot listening the best he could while pretending to wait on the other customers, finally sat down at the table and said "OK, fill me in."

"Excuse us," I said. "Police business."

"Aw, give me a break. The council has been on me for weeks to find out if you're making any progress."

"We're making progress. We're just methodical."

He snickered. "Oh, haha. If I was as methodical as you, my customers would die of starvation. So what's the deal? Who did it?"

"If I tell you, you'll keep it quiet? You can't tell the council."

He nodded, trying to look as somber as possible.

I told him about the clue and the Bible verse. Matthew 9:5. "For which is easier, to say 'your sins are forgiven,' or to say 'Rise, and walk?'"

"So who is it?" he asked, not understanding.

"Well, according to the clue, which may or may not point to the real killer, the murderer is Rhiza Walker."

He looked confused for a moment. But only for a moment.

"Ah...rise and walk." He nodded his approval. "Very clever."

Dave and Nancy looked at each other and I saw Nancy's eyes roll ever so slightly heavenward.

"You can't say anything to anyone," I admonished. "It would hamper the investigation."

"I won't tell a soul."

We all knew he was lying. Oh, he'd try not to tell but Nancy, Dave and I—even Pete himself—knew that he had the biggest mouth on this side of the Cumberland Gap. That, coupled with the fact that I had told Marilyn, the church secretary, almost guaranteed that I'd be having a meeting with Rhiza and or Malcolm before the afternoon was over. Which is what I wanted.

Back at the station, I had Dave run the phone records on the Walker's home and cell phones. Malcolm had a satellite phone, which I also had Dave run a trace on. A half hour later, I had a list of every call they had made for a week on either side of the murder—specifically, every call they had made to Loraine Ryan's home and cell phone. They may have had a good reason for calling her at home. But forty-seven phone calls in three days? I doubted it.

I walked into choir rehearsal to an impromptu performance of one of my finer dramatic musical works. Actually, the BRAs had gotten there early to inaugurate a new choir member who, when I walked in, happened to be almost on the floor in hysterical laughter. The offending work was one of my Epiphany musicals concerning the Three Queens of Orient. In my own defense, these were written for choir parties and weren't scheduled for liturgical performance.

The Three Kings, being acted by Bob Solomon, Sammy Royce and Fred May, all reading from the script with great declaration and verisimilitude, meet at the beginning of the play and decide to take their gifts to the newborn king, who they are sure has been born directly under a very bright star in the East.

After they leave posthaste, the three queens, named Leona, Imelda and Hillary, get together to discuss what is to be done while the Kings are on their journey. Leona is the mean, bossy soprano who keeps having all her servants executed for failing to keep the bathroom clean. Imelda is the large alto who needs a small caravan just to carry her shoes. Hillary, the savvy mezzo who made her fortune in illegal inside camel trading, points out that since these kings are already from the Orient, if they follow a star in the East for any length of time, they'll end up in the Pacific Ocean.

I must say here that the work includes many beautiful arias including the Song of the Lowly Handmaiden,

I know I'm just a concubine,
But won't you be my valentine?

There's also the most famous of the trios which the ladies were currently singing with great glee.

We three Queens of Orient are
All our husbands followed the star
They thought it was mannish,
But they don't speak Spanish,
They probably won't get far. Ohh-ohhhh.
Star of wonder, star so blessed;
Shining in the East celeste.
So we ponder as they wander,
Why on earth did they go West?

I'm Leona, bitter as gall,
I can cause a terrible squall,
Rich as Midas, star to guide us,
I am the queen of all. Ohh-ohhhh.
Star of wonder, star so keen,
But I'm the biggest star you've seen.
We'll travel slowly, tax the lowly,
'Cause I am the Queen of Mean.

I'm Imelda, jolly and quaint,
Rather large, a face like a saint,
My shoes I can carry, on one dromedary,
If I show real restraint. Ohh-ohhhh.
Star of wonder, star most fair,
I'm wandering without footwear.
It may seem callous, but at my palace
I have around three thousand pair.

I am Hillary, savvy and wise,
My king has some wandering eyes,
But if I scare him in the harem
He'll get a real surprise! Ohh-ohhhh.
I have traveled from afar
Following my husband's star
When I squeezed him if I'd pleased him,
He said, "Close, but no cigar."

The choir finished up with a rousing chorus and applauded themselves mightily.

"Hayden, this is Rebecca Watts," said Georgia seeing me come in. "She's a new alto."

"Well, she won't last too long in this choir if you treat her like this."

"No, no. I love it." said Rebecca. "It's the best choir rehearsal I've ever been to."

"It's a pleasure to have you with us," I said in my best 'welcome-to-the-choir' voice. "Did you get a folder?"

"We were planning to sing *The Weasel Cantata* next," said Marjorie.

"Maybe later," I said putting her off. "We have to hit the Charpentier *Midnight Mass* pretty hard this evening."

After the rehearsal, I checked my pager. Sure enough, there were two calls from Rhiza and three from Malcolm. I'd get to them tomorrow morning. I was beat and I still had to feed Archimedes.

I began the next morning with a cup of coffee and the Vince Guaraldi Trio playing the soundtrack from *A Charlie Brown Christmas*. I followed my coffee up with a couple of phone calls. I was contemplating getting a new 100 CD changer that I saw in a catalog, hooking it up to the stereo and putting in a hundred Christmas CDs to capture that Christmas spirit that had been lacking of late. Here it was, mid-December and I still hadn't put up my tree. Meg and I had planned to go out to the tree farm later this afternoon, but she had canceled due to a client in a panic about his 401k.

My first call was to Malcolm Walker's satellite phone. There was no answer which, in itself, was odd. Malcolm always answered his phone and with a satellite phone, he was never out of range. My next call was to Rhiza's cell. She answered on the first ring.

"Hi Rhiza. It's Hayden."

"Hayden, thank God."

"What's wrong?" I asked. I hadn't expected such a panicked reply.

"Everything is wrong. I don't know what to do."

"Why don't you come over and see me. I'm at the house."

"Malcolm left last night and didn't come home. I don't know where he is and he won't answer his phone."

"I know. I just tried him."

"I'll be over in a little bit," she said and hung up.

I spent the next hour going through my music collection, trying to pick the top hundred Christmas CDs. I admit I have a rather large CD collection. Well, four or five thousand anyway. I join music clubs regularly and just have them send their monthly offering, which my accountant pays as a matter of course. Then, when I'm at Tower Records, I'll buy a couple of dozen recordings that catch my eye. One thing I did spend some money on, after I had become flush, was trading in my vinyl for CDs. I still kept the vinyl recordings—in some ways the sound is much better—but if I found one that I couldn't replace or duplicate with a CD from the record label, I paid a student at Appalachian State to transfer it for me.

Rhiza knocked on the door and opened it in the same motion just as she had always done. I didn't mind. We were old friends.

"C'mon in," I called from the kitchen. "I'll bring some coffee."

"Thanks." She plopped down in my reading chair as she had a hundred times before, letting the leather and overstuffed cushions catch her as she dropped. I had seen her look better. "Haggard" was probably a good word to describe her. She was wearing an old pair of jeans and a sweatshirt. No makeup. Not exactly the Rhiza I was used to seeing around town for the past few years. Make no mistake; she was still a knockout. In a lot of ways, to my eye anyway, more appealing in her natural state than in the trophy wife getup.

Rhiza and I had a history. She was quite a clever girl and when she dropped the husky-squeaky voice that enraptured Malcolm in favor of her gentle North Carolina mountain accent, her whole personality changed for the better.

"Put on a Mozart symphony, will you?" she asked. "Number 26 if you can find it. God, I get so tired of listening to Mannheim Steamroller all Christmas long."

She hopped up, went over to the humidor, took out one of my R&J's, snipped off the end and lit it up. She fell back into the feather cushions, puffing on the cigar, and draping a long leg over the arm of the chair. On her, I have to admit, that cigar looked good.

I found the Mozart CD and replaced Charlie Brown jazz with the Viennese classical.

"In our house it's either Mannheim Steamroller or Windham Hill from Thanksgiving to New Years. What did Doonesbury call it? Air Pudding. It makes me want to become a brunette again," she said as I handed her a cup of coffee.

I had first met Rhiza at Chapel Hill when I was a grad student and she was a freshman. She was a music history major and we hit it off right away. In fact, it was Rhiza and Pete who had called me about the job in St. Germaine after I found my second career. When I met her in grad school, she was a decent pianist with no illusions about a professional career. She was on a teaching track and doing some good research on folk music of the Outer Banks. She was also a brunette, drop-dead gorgeous, and quite interested in consciousness altering experiences of various kinds—musical, chemical, and sexual. I must admit, she had aged more gracefully than I. If anything, she was more beautiful now than she had been then. I was pretty sure that no one in town knew about us, although she continued to drop by the cabin until she got hooked up with Malcolm five years ago. Now she stopped in occasionally for some coffee and to chat, but she didn't drop by. I'm sure Meg didn't know about our background, and since we didn't ever discuss our ancient history, I didn't feel guilty about not telling her.

"I didn't do it," she said, sipping her coffee, the cigar dangling in her other hand while the strains of Mozart 26 filled the room. "You've got to believe me."

Her eyes were smoldering--smoldering as the passion which hung heavilly in the room like some gigantic velvet curtain smothering the atmosphere. My gaze followed the thin wisp of smoke from the cigar dangling like an extra

appendage from her delicate, well-manicured hand. Yep.
They always came to me for help.

It was déjà vu all over again.

Chapter 16

"I didn't do it. You know I couldn't have, " Rhiza said. "I can't believe it's all over town."

"What's all over town?"

"The rumor. Apparently there's a clue that says I did it. I'm the murderer."

The town grapevine was more effective than I'd thought. It hadn't even been twenty-four hours.

"Well, we do have a clue and it does point to you," I told her honestly. There was no point in lying to her at this stage.

"What's the clue?" she asked. "Can I see it?"

"I have a copy of it here somewhere. The original's down at the station." I started rummaging through papers on the table, which were stacking up at an alarming rate. I found the Xerox as Mozart's 26th moved into the slow movement and handed it over to her. She chomped down on the cigar, freeing up her non-coffee hand and gave the note a quick read.

"What the hell does *this* mean?"

She stared at me while I went through all the permutations of the anagram, the hymn numbers and the Bible passages, finally ending with "Rise and walk."

"That's it? That's the clue?"

"I admit it's weak," I said, sitting down on the couch. "And it doesn't really point to anyone specifically."

"You're damn right it doesn't. Why didn't you just call me and ask me?" Rhiza was a little chapped. "Malcolm is fit to be tied. He took off yesterday and I haven't been able to get in touch with him."

"OK, now I'm asking. Why would someone leave an obscure clue to the murder pointing to you? What's going on? And don't tell me you don't know what I'm talking about."

She looked at me for a long moment. "Do you ever think about me, you know, dropping by?" she asked, using our euphemism.

"Yeah, I do," I said. "Sometimes. But I'm semi-attached, and you're permanently attached. That's not trouble we want."

"Nobody would have to know."

"I appreciate the offer, madam, but I'm afraid I must decline," I said, trying my best to make a quick joke out of the invitation. I wasn't at all sure that she was serious, but we had enough history to make me think she was.

Rhiza nodded and smiled a sad smile. "You're a good guy, Hayden. That's the problem." She got up, walked over to the fireplace and tossed in the half-smoked cigar. "Malcolm's having an affair."

I tried not to look surprised, although news like that always catches me off guard.

"Do you know who?" I asked.

"Yep."

I waited for the other shoe to drop.

"Loraine Ryan."

When I thought about it, Mother Ryan would not be considered unattractive by most of the male population of St. Germaine. She wasn't a beauty queen by any means, but she had a look about her, a look my old music department chairman used to call "bedroom eyes." She was an ash-blonde with shoulder length hair, fairly slim, and had a nice figure. In fact, when she showed up at St. Barnabas, I remember thinking, lecher that I am, that working with a lady priest wouldn't be half bad. That is, until she opened her mouth. Then, for me at least, the magic was gone.

"Loraine and Malcolm? Are you sure?"

"I think so."

"I always assumed that, being an unmarried militant feminist—well—that she 'danced at the other end of the ballroom,' if you get my meaning."

"I'm pretty sure that she dances at *both* ends, if you get mine."

"Wow," I said, caught off guard by this particular revelation. I must have sat there in stunned silence for a good thirty seconds before blurting out, "Wanna feed my owl?"

She laughed for the first time, that wonderful laugh that sounded like bells. "OK, Romeo, but that's the first time I've heard it called *that*."

"No, really. I've got an owl in the kitchen. C'mon."

One thing you could never say about Rhiza was that she was squeamish. She had grown up in the mountains and whatever pretensions she had put on for Malcolm's benefit disappeared when she reached into the coffee can and came out with two dead mice. I opened the kitchen window and about twenty seconds later Archimedes stepped through.

"No *WAY!* This is so cool!"

I could see she was impressed. "He used to take about ten minutes to notice the window was open. Now he spots it almost immediately."

"You don't think he's becoming dependent, do you?"

"I don't think so. We don't feed him enough. A couple of mice a day. He's got to eat more than that to stay alive. It's just a mousy supplement."

Archimedes took both the offerings from our hands and left just as quickly as he came.

As I waited my turn to wash my hands in the kitchen sink, Rhiza said, "So what do I do now?"

"I don't know. I sure am sorry to hear about Malcolm, but I need to figure out this clue. Why would anyone go to all this trouble to point the finger at you? It doesn't make any sense."

"No it doesn't. Is there any other evidence?" She finished up and was drying her hands leaving the water running for me to wash.

"Not really. A lot of...stuff. Circumstantial. I sure would like to know who did it though."

"I really love Malcolm. He's, well, he's comfortable," she said, finally finding the right word. "I wish we hadn't gotten involved

178

with that woman, but he's Senior Warden, y'know? Someone had to be nice to her. Almost everyone else hates her guts."

I, being a sensitive kind of guy, didn't add, "With good reason."

"Look, Rhiza," I said finally, "she's not a nice person and as a priest, she's a disaster."

"I know. I'm not a complete fool. But Malcolm liked her from the beginning. He was always in her office – meetings in the mornings and late at night. I don't know what to do."

"How do you know he's having an affair?"

"I heard one of the voice mail messages on his sat-phone. He hadn't erased it because he hadn't heard it. And he *doesn't* know that *I* heard it."

"What did it say?"

"Hello darling. Call me."

"That's it? And you call *my* evidence weak?"

"It's enough. I know her voice. I ought to."

Six hours later I pulled up in Meg's drive, got out of the truck and gallantly opened the door for her to climb aboard. First to dinner, then a movie. I even wore my new mock-turtle neck.

"Hayden, Can we please take *my* car?"

"Do I get to drive?" I asked.

"Oh, I insist."

On the way into Boone we listened to the Vaughan Williams' *Hodie* and I gave Megan the highlights of Rhiza's visit. Well, if not the highlights, the parts about Malcolm and Herself.

"I don't believe it. Malcolm and Loraine?"

"My thoughts exactly. But there's something else going on." I broke out my best Alfred Hitchcock voice. "Even now, all is not as it seems."

"You'll let me know if something else happens, right? This is really getting interesting. I may have to write my own book."

"Consider it done."

Chapter 17

"This is going to be a pleasure," said a sadistic, very
low, and only slightly feminine voice. Denver Tweed moved
toward me like a schoolyard bully after a sixth grade
violinist. Her head was pulled down into her shoulders like
a demented tortoise, making what little neck she had disappear entirely, her massive hands clenching and
unclenching as she measured the damage her country ham
fists would do to me. I backed into the bookcase. There was
nowhere to run.

Amber Dawn, Personal Trainer, and Isabel watched with
amusement. I could see that Amber still had her gun
trained on me, but Ms. Tweed's corpus magnum was beginning
to block out the rest of the room. I figured my odds were
about as good as those of a floral design consultant in a
biker bar.

I took a chance and threw the first punch, a looping
right hand which glanced off her head, doing no real
damage. Her chin was buried deep into her shoulder blades,
but I could see her cold smile as she raised her fists high
in response to the blow. Her black, beady eyes locked on
mine and she moved in close, pinning me against the shelf.
She didn't fake a punch--she just hit me. She hit me high.
She hit me low. Too low. Then everything went black.

When the haze finally began to lift, I saw Denver,
Amber and Isabel ransacking my office. Every book had
been pulled off the shelves, all the drawers emptied and
dumped unceremoniously in the middle of the room, the rugs
pulled up and the pictures yanked off the walls. My office
was beginning to resemble my old apartment. They had found
my wall safe, which was hidden behind a portrait of J.
Edgar Hoover's mother, and were working on opening it.
From my fetal position, I reached to my ankle holster and

pulled a small Taurus .38 special from its hiding place. It was small, but packed a wallop. I hoped it was enough.

The morning brought the first snowfall of the season. Pristine and sparkling, it covered the view in every direction. I dropped the old truck into four-wheel drive, just in case I needed the traction, and headed in toward town, taking the winding highway at a nice, slow pace, enjoying the scenery as well as being particularly careful. In my experience, most of the winter accidents in St. Germaine happened during or right after the first snowfall. Many times, here in the mountains, the snow was just a powdered sugar sprinkling over a cake of solid ice.

Meg and I had rescheduled our Christmas tree outing for the afternoon, barring any unforeseen police or financial crisis. If the cold and slightly overcast weather held, this would be a fine time to pick out a tree. With the snow hanging on the branches, we wouldn't even have to imagine the finished product.

After a quick stop at The Slab for a Danish to go and brief holiday salutations to Pete and Bob Solomon, I was off to the station for a few phone calls. The first was to Dr. Dougherty, the local GP.

"Hi Karen. Hayden Konig." I said, once I had sweet-talked my way past the receptionist.

"How are you, Hayden?" she said. Karen Dougherty was a pediatrician before she retired and after moving to St. Germaine, worked a couple of days a week as the one and only practitioner of the medical arts in town. Almost everyone with an emergency or who visited a doctor on a regular basis went into Boone, but Dr. Dougherty was happy to do well-baby checkups, routine vaccinations, flu shots and the like.

"I'm fine, Karen. I just have a question."

"Shoot."

"Did you ever see Willie Boyd? I mean, on a professional basis."

"He did stop in once a couple of years ago. If I remember correctly, he was complaining of chest pain. Let me look."

While I was on hold, I took the opportunity to rummage around on the top of my desk and find a pen and a pad of paper, vowing once again to clean up my desk, or at least to have someone else do it.

"Got it," she said, coming back to the phone. "Hmmm," she said, using the doctor's familiar "hmmm," which they are all taught in the first year of medical school. "I listened to his chest and then sent him down to the free clinic in Boone. That's all I've got. No follow-up. They didn't call me, so I presume they took care of it."

"Do you have a number for the clinic?"

"I'll give you back to Polly. She'll get you what you need."

After thanking her and getting the phone number from Polly, my next call was to the clinic in Boone.

The *Crèches of St. Germaine*, as the event was being advertised in the *Watauga Democrat*, was scheduled to kickoff on December 18th at 7:00 in the evening. The forecast was for snow and an Arctic front, which was nice for the Christmas ambiance, but terrible for the relatively scantily clad angels who had to endure the single-digit temperatures for an hour and a half. There was some talk at The Slab about cutting the time down from an hour-and-a-half to an hour, but neither organization was ready to give an inch. The First Baptist Church Elder Adult Handbell Choir, known as the *Nana Pealers*, if you could believe their monogrammed, sky-blue windsuits, was scheduled to play at the Kiwanis display for the first half hour. The Rotarians, trying for a quick *coup de gras*, had hired a brass quintet from the university, but yesterday, after seeing the weather projection, they had called and canceled, explaining that their mouthpieces would freeze to their lips.

"We're in trouble," Bob Solomon told Pete as I waited in line to pay for my Danish. "The brass players are wimping out."

"The temperature will be nine degrees without the wind chill. I hardly call that wimping out," said Pete as he rang up Bob's breakfast tab.

"Anyway, we have a backup plan. I got in touch with a guy who lives up on Grandfather Mountain. He's a bagpiper."

"That sounds pretty good."

"He says he can play some Christmas songs, but he's wearing his red longjohns under his kilt."

I put my two dollars on the counter and escaped without being asked to comment.

"This is Detective Konig of the St. Germaine Police Department," I said, identifying myself to the doctor on duty at the St. Luke Free Clinic in Boone. "To whom am I speaking?"

"Hello, Detective. This is Dr. Drummond. What can I do for you?"

"You had a patient named William Boyd. He would have been coming in for the past two years."

"I don't remember the name, but there are quite a few doctors that volunteer their time at the clinic."

"Would he have seen anyone on a regular basis?"

"I doubt it," Dr. Drummond said. "He would have to see whoever was on duty. We don't make appointments with specific doctors."

"Would he have a chart that I could look at?"

"Of course. But I can't let you see it without his permission."

"Yes, well that's the problem. He dead."

"Next of kin?" Dr. Drummond asked.

"None that we can find."

"Well, fax me over a death certificate and I'll send the chart over."

"I have the number, but I'll come by and pick it up, if that's OK?"

"It'll be ready for you at the desk. But fax the death certificate," he reiterated.

"It's on the way. Thanks, Doctor."

I was on my way to Boone to pick up Willie Boyd's file when my pager went off. It was Malcolm. My plan was to drop by Kent Murphee's office on my way home, ask him about the file and deliver a Christmas present. Having done the autopsy, I thought that Kent might be able to give me some insight. I decided Malcolm could wait.

Willie's chart was waiting for me at the desk as promised and I was on my way to the coroner's office after stopping by Starbucks for a couple of espressos. One for me, one for Kent—whether he wanted it or not.

"Bourbon?" he asked, as soon as I walked in. I may have been becoming a little too predictable.

"Sheesh, Kent. It's 10:00 in the morning. At least we can *pretend* that we're being civilized. Pour mine into this coffee." I pushed his espresso across the desk to him and he poured a couple of fingers into both cups.

"Cheers," he said, picking up the file folder with his free hand and leaning back in his chair.

I stirred my coffee with the end of my pen, wiped it on my jacket and waited for Kent to peruse the file.

"Looks like your boy had a bum ticker. But I knew that already."

"You knew? Why didn't you tell me?"

"It didn't really have anything to do with the autopsy. He still died of poison. Having a bad heart, it may have taken less to kill him, but he had a dose that would have killed three men. Anyway, it was in the report. 'Signs of heart disease.' Didn't you read it?"

"I'm ashamed to say that I must have missed it. How bad was he?"

"Bad enough. Congestive heart disease. He probably had three months, six at the most. He might have been a candidate for a bypass five or six years ago, but he was way past that.

"Did he know? I mean, did the doctor tell him?"

"Yep," he said flipping the page. "He knew."

"Do me a favor, will you?"

"Sure, since it's Christmas and I'm feeling pretty generous. Also, may I expect the usual Christmas gift from the St. Germaine PD?" referring to the case of bourbon I'd been taking up the past few years. "Not that I need the bribe. I only ask because they're having a sale down at Appalachian Liquors and if you're sending something special, I won't go down and stock up."

"I have your gift in the back of the truck."

"You are a gentleman and a scholar."

"Now the favor," I said, pulling a baggie out of my pocket containing a cheap, half-smoked cigar.

I was coming back into town when my pager went off again. Malcolm Walker three times in the last hour. I knew he was getting pretty worried when I walked into the station to a chorus of "Mr. Walker has been calling all morning. He's on the line now." I nodded, grabbed a donut off the counter and headed into my office, closing the door behind me and picking up the phone.

"Hi, Malcolm, it's me," I said.

"Hayden. Thank God. We've got to talk." Malcolm sounded past worried and well on the way to frantic.

"Calm down. I can meet you right now if you want."

"Yes, of course I do. Can you come by the office?"

"No problem. I'll be there in five minutes."

"Anything going on?" I asked Dave as I went back though the office on my way out, my iBook in my hand. I had thought seriously about getting a case for it, but it was easier to just haul it around with me.

"Nope," said Dave. "But don't forget the show tonight. *The Crèches of St. Germaine.* Sounds pretty poetic."

"What's the forecast? How cold is it supposed to be?"

"About six degrees by showtime. Some light snow."

"I'll bundle up. You coming?"

"I wouldn't miss it," Dave said, laughing. "Nancy'll be there too. We figured a show of force would be the best deterrent to the Christmas looting."

"Very funny."

Malcolm was expecting me. I met Mona, his secretary, leaving the office, taking what she called "an early lunch." Mona, unlike Rhiza, his former secretary turned wife, was in her late 50's and gave the word "frumpy" a whole new meaning. I suspected that Rhiza had a hand in the hiring.

"Come on in Hayden. Want a drink?"

"No thanks, I've already had my limit this morning."

Looking slightly puzzled but not saying anything else, Malcolm ushered me into his office and closed the door. I'd been in here many times before. The look was what we in the biz call "well-appointed." Not overdone opulence, but sparsely elegant with only the best in furnishings. There wasn't a piece of furniture in this office that cost less than four thousand dollars, and I suspected most were several times that figure. I knew for a fact that he paid over fifty thousand dollars just for the carpet because I was at the same auction and ended up with a twelve-hundred-dollar antique sleigh bed. Of course, as he pointed out later, his purchase was tax deductible. Mine was not. I suspected, although I did not know for sure, that the Andrew Wyeth water color on the wall was an original. The three leather club chairs and the sofa in the seating area came from a 19th-century gentleman's club in France that had sold its furnishings when it was closed by the government in the 1980's for offering a little more female companionship than was mentioned in the membership brochure. A small LCD computer screen and a keyboard perched on top of and off to one side of his antique mahogany desk. A couple of antique Montblanc fountain pens finished the desktop. There were some papers—I assumed financial reports—neatly stacked on the opposite corner. His bookshelves were neat and well ordered, as if the books were a just prop in his set dressing and I had my doubts that few if any of them had been opened. There was a wet bar against the far wall and as he motioned me to a leather chair in the informal seating area, he went to over to it and poured himself a glass of something to steel his nerves.

"You've heard the rumors?" he said, finishing his drink in two gulps and taking a seat across from me.

"A few. What did *you* hear?" I asked him.

"I heard what everyone else has heard," he said trying to control his obvious anger. "Loraine Ryan said that you'd deciphered the clue and that it pointed to Rhiza."

"Well, yes," I admitted. "It does point to Rhiza, but it's not definitive by any means. It could have been written by anyone."

"What is it that you *do* know, if I may ask?"

"You may," I answered, putting the laptop on the coffee table between us and opening it up.

"You certainly have gone high tech lately," Malcolm commented with no real interest as the screen glowed to life.

"Yep, Kicking and screaming into the twenty-first century. Here's what I have."

I went through the litany again for myself as well as Malcolm, hoping something would jump out at me. I didn't share all my thoughts with Mr. Walker, but I did give him the highlights.

Willie Boyd was killed on Friday afternoon a little after five. He called the police station at 5:10 to report a robbery—a robbery that he himself had committed. He was found at 5:17. We found the three cases of wine in the trunk of his car. He had taken Loraine Ryan's cross from the sacristy and, according to Bev, who was in

187

the sacristy and saw him, kissed it before going up to the choir loft where he then drank some of the wine he had stolen. Then he had a heart attack and died. The wine was not poisoned as first believed, but the cross was loaded with chemicals from the oleander plant. The chemicals were absorbed though Willie Boyd's oral membranes. The olive-wood cross from the Holy Land was the murder weapon.

There was a clue to the murder left on the organ by someone still unknown.

I saw who did it. It's Him. It's Matthew.
O hark the herald angels sing;
The boy's descent which lifted up the world;

The clue points to a bible verse—Matthew 9:5. "For which is easier, to say 'your sins are forgiven,' or to say 'Rise, and walk?" This clue seems to point to Rhiza Walker. But it's weak. Very weak.

I'm was pretty sure that Willie's death was an accident and that the cross was intended for Loraine Ryan. After all, it is the priest's custom to kiss the cross they wear as they place it around their neck. If it didn't kill Loraine immediately, it would surely make her very sick, and eventually Herself would have gotten a fatal dose. The cross was boiled in the oleander and was lethal. There wasn't any way that the murderer would know that Willie would steal the cross or that he had a bad heart. The dose that killed him probably wouldn't have killed a healthy person on the first try.

I also suspect that Mother Ryan knew more than she was saying. She was in the kitchen and knew about the oleander broth that JJ had been cooking up for the hedgehogs.

So, I was back to the question "who would want Loraine Ryan dead?" With Rhiza's recent revelations, I was ready to look seriously at the man sitting across from me.

Malcolm studied me without saying anything for a long moment.

"How well do you know Rhiza?"

"Oh, I don't know," I shrugged, trying to avoid answering the question and hoping he wouldn't press the issue. The truth was, I knew her very well.

He got up, went over to the bar and poured himself another drink. His back was to me when I heard him say, "She's having an affair."

I processed the comment, made sure I heard correctly, then said "Really? I'm sorry." I waited the appropriate ten seconds for him to say something: then I ventured "Any idea who?"

"Yes. I know who."

I waited again as he turned around and looked at me, a sad look in his eyes.

"It's Loraine. Loraine Ryan."

What was it that Rhiza said? "I'm pretty sure she dances at *both* ends of the ballroom."

"Are you sure?" I asked Malcolm.

"Pretty sure. At least as sure as I can be without walking in on them."

"How do you know?"

"Notes, messages. She's in Loraine's office at all hours of the night. And now this." He handed me a piece of folded paper. I opened it and read the handwritten message aloud.

"Darling—meet me in my office after eight."

"You know who wrote it?"

"It's Loraine's handwriting. I've seen it plenty of times."

"Well, maybe it wasn't Rhiza's note," I offered.

"It was in her coat pocket. Please," he begged. "Don't say anything to anyone."

I didn't know what to say.

"I always knew she was...that Rhiza was...hmm...attracted to women." He continued, searching for the right words. "I just knew," he said finally. "She was always hanging around Loraine. Going into her office for meetings at all hours, taking notes for her conference." He drained his glass for the second time. "But I don't think Rhiza tried to kill her."

I was on the phone about thirty seconds after I got back to the office. No sense in beating about the bush.

"Hello, Rhiza? It's Hayden."

"Hayden. What a surprise."

"Knock it off." I admit I was more than a little irked at the way she played me. "I just talked to Malcolm."

"Thank God. He still won't call me back. Where is he?" She actually sounded concerned.

I cut right to the chase. "He says you're having an affair with Loraine Ryan."

Silence.

"Did you hear me? I said–"

"I heard you."

More silence.

"Rhiza? You still there?"

"Oh, hell. Did he say how he found out? Did he say it was from Willie?"

Now it was my turn to bite my tongue.

"We need to talk," I said, meaning "I need to think for a bit."

"Tonight?" she asked.

"No. I've got to police the show. Come on over tomorrow morning. Around nine."

"I'll be there in time for coffee."

Chapter 18

"I think that's about enough," I said, sitting up and spitting a few teeth onto the wooden floor like so many unchewed tic-tacs. I waved my .38 at the three them as menacingly as I could, noting that Amber's gun was resting safely on my desk a good two giant steps from any of the so-called ladies in the room.

Denver Tweed took one look at my weapon and let out a walrus-like bark that I took to be some kind of laughter.

"Who do you think you're going to stop with that peashooter?" she growled, cracking her knuckles and flexing her thumbs in anticipation.

I looked at Denver and stopped waving the gun, pointing it instead at Amber Dawn.

"Not you, Denver, certainly," I said, getting to my feet. "But I'll be more than happy to make Amber Dawn a lot less attractive real fast."

Denver didn't take my meaning and started toward me to finish the job she started. I pulled the hammer back on the .38, cocked it and leveled it squarely at Amber's face. I didn't know if I could do it, but if not, I was going to play the bluff to the bitter end.

"Stop!" shouted Isabel. Denver looked back at her, puzzled as a gorilla in one of those wax banana factories.

I had figured there was more to Isabel and Amber's relationship than met the eye and that Isabel wasn't about to sacrifice her to a beat up gumshoe.

"I can finish him," growled Denver.

"Maybe," I said, "maybe not. I might get off one shot, maybe two. Either way, someone besides me is goin' out of here feet first." I spit out another tic-tac.

"Now what?" said Isabel, her eyes as narrow as Jimmy Swaggart's theology.

I pulled some handcuffs from my back pocket and tossed them to her.

"Now you cuff your goon to the piano." I kept my eyes on Denver but my gun was still pointed at Amber's lovely visage. Isabel pulled Denver back across the room and cuffed her wrist to the leg of the upright.

Suddenly Amber lunged for the gun on the desk. Isabel dropped down onto one knee in a classic shooting stance, bringing up a heretofore hidden automatic of her own. Denver heaved toward me with the piano in tow like a Clydesdale pulling a beer truck.

That's when the fun started.

"Hmmm, what's that?" asked Meg, climbing into the truck and commenting on the music. This was one of the few times I could remember that she didn't have a disparaging comment about my mode of transport, probably because we were off to the Pine Valley Christmas Tree Farm and could use the four-wheel drive, but also due to the fact that the heater had stopped working in her Lexus and at three o'clock the temperature was eighteen degrees and dropping.

"*A Renaissance Christmas.* The Waverly Consort."

"It's beautiful."

"I've had the album since college, but I just now found it on CD. When are you getting your heater fixed?" I asked.

"I have to take it in to Asheville tomorrow morning. There's no one around here to do warranty work. They'll give me a loaner."

"Ah," I said, mentally checking my apprehension about having Rhiza visit the house tomorrow morning.

We drove up to the Pine Valley Christmas Tree Farm to the sounds of Renaissance Christmas carols and a few unaccompanied motets of Palestrina. I was definitely feeling the spirit of the season by the time we reached the snow covered rows of seven foot tall blue spruce—my personal favorite. Meg and her mother had put their tree up weeks ago and by Christmas it would be hanging on to its remaining needles like grim death. I liked my trees fresh, preferring to get them later in the season and leave them up until January sixth, Epiphany being the traditional end to the twelve days of Christmas.

We parked and went inside the cabin that served as the sales office. There was a fire blazing in the old stone fireplace and Ardine McCollough was sitting on the couch in front of the fire with an afghan draped over her shoulders reading a magazine. She got up and greeted us as we shook the snow from our boots.

"I hope y'all dressed warm."

"We did indeed," said Meg.

"Do you want to pick one out? I can come and cut it down for you if you want. There hasn't been many folks out here the last few days. Everybody's got their trees by now I 'spect."

"I've got a saw. You just wait here," I told her. "It's pretty cold out there. You have any matches?"

"I sure don't. You know, we had some books printed up a couple years ago, but they've been gone since I-don't-know-when. Nothin's gonna burn out there anyway. I got a lighter, if you want it."

I shook my head. "No thanks."

"You want a blue spruce? The six-foot trees are sixty, the seven-footers are eighty. If you want an eight-footer I can give it to you for forty-five. Next year they'll be too big to sell and we'll have to make wreaths out of them."

"I'll get an eight-footer then."

"They're down the hill in the far lot. Drive on down past the pond, turn right and you'll see them there on the left. There aren't a whole lot left, but they're all pretty."

"You're going to need some more Christmas lights," Meg quipped, heading for the door and pulling her cap down around her ears.

We found our tree in short order, cut it down with the chainsaw I had put in the back of the truck, loaded it up and were heading back to the cabin to pay Ardine—all in about twenty minutes. I suspected that the tree was closer to nine feet than eight, but I had the room and I figured that the owner wouldn't mind too much.

I paid Ardine the forty-five dollars and mentioned that I'd be by on Christmas Eve with some presents for the kids. She nodded and smiled gratefully. I'd been their Santa Claus for the past four or five years.

It was already dark when we got to the cabin. We spent the next hour getting it in the stand, set in the living room and tied off to the walls. It was Meg who suggested we head for town.

"We don't want to be late for *The Crèches of St. Germaine*."

"We don't want to be early either. It's down to six degrees."

"At least your heater works."

We pulled up to the police station and parked in my reserved spot. It was only a couple blocks from the festivities and if worse came to worst, we could duck into the station to warm up. Apparently the rest of the crowd wasn't as worried about the cold weather. There were at least a couple of hundred people chatting, singing carols and braving the cold and the snow, which was starting to come down steadily. Everyone was bundled up, having a good time and the holiday spirit seemed to be pervasive.

At seven on the dot, the back door of the Rotarian display opened up and the players got into position. The displays were static—that is, the players struck a tableau and stood there for the entire hour-and-a-half while music played in the background. The public wasn't expected to stay for the entire time—just as long as it took to get the *Weinachtsgeist*, the Christmas Spirit— so mothers weren't too worried about their kids getting frostbite.

The characters, however, would be feeling the cold pretty fiercely in about twenty minutes.

"How long do we have to stay?" asked Meg, already feeling a little chilled despite the silk long underwear, two sweaters, an insulated ski suit, a coat, a fur hat with ear flaps and electric socks and gloves.

"Till the bitter end."

The Kiwanians were in position shortly after seven. They had built a small petting zoo that contained a miniature donkey, a calf, two lambs, a llama and a St. Bernard puppy named Bertram. There was a veterinarian dressed in ancient Hebrew garb who had been with the animals since six in case the kids wanted to come early and see them. By seven, the calf was starting to show some distress and one of the lambs had gone to sleep and wouldn't wake up, so the vet had taken them all back to his heated van, except the llama and the puppy, who was apparently very excited and in his element.

The *Nana Pealers*, Senior Adult Handbell choir from the Baptist Church, had gotten there at about a quarter till seven and set up their handbell tables to the side of the Kiwanian crèche. The wind was beginning to pick up and the Kiwanians, being on the north side facing south, were going to get the worst of it.

At about five after seven, the handbell choir was ready to play and most of the crowd had moved to the north side of the street. Apparently the ringers had their music memorized because they weren't using any scores. There was a number of bells placed on the tables in front of the choir as well as two, three, or in some cases four bells in each of the players hands. They started playing a lively arrangement of *The Carol of the Bells* and were about thirty seconds into the piece when the first bell shattered.

It didn't make a loud sound. Just a dull 'clink' as the bell broke in half. In the next ten seconds, twelve more bells cracked before the director realized what was happening and stopped the performance. With frozen tears in her eyes, she muttered an apology

195

and the choir started packing up their equipment.

Across the street, the Rotarians and their cast were poised in position. The effect was stunning. The snow was falling harder now and Mrs. Horst, portraying the innkeeper's wife, was on the balcony in a welcoming pose beckoning all who were weary and heavy laden to come in to the warmth of the stable. But Mrs. Horst's lips were quickly turning blue.

The Rotarians' bagpiper showed up at about ten after seven, got his pipes out, gave a couple of preliminary honks and then took off on the bagpipe version of *Frosty The Snowman*. This caused Seymour Krebbs' camel, an adolescent last year, but this year a full grown bull, to look around the stable and try to find just what or who was bellowing the mating call of the dromedary.

When the first drone of the pipes had begun to sound, the crowd had moved from the angelic clanking of the breaking bells, across the street to the dulcet tones of a bagpipe and the artistic bellowing of a camel in heat. Joseph and Mary were glancing nervously across the stable, showing absolutely no parental loyalty to the 40 watt light bulb glowing reverently in the manger. They were trying to hold their nativic poses and not bolt and run. The shepherds, most of whom were teenaged boys, had huddled against one of the walls, their eyes looking for a quick and unobtrusive escape.

Seymour was hanging onto the halter of the beast, trying his best to pull it back out of the stable, but to no avail. He was little more than an irritation.

"Don't shoot the camel," Meg said. "It's not his fault."

I didn't want to shoot the camel, but I wouldn't have minded shooting the bagpiper if I had to.

Two more shepherdic Rotarians from the plains of Judea had grabbed onto the camel's halter and the animal was having a bit more trouble slinging the combined weight of the three men around the stable than it did tossing Seymour. Another of the club members had finally tackled the piper just as he got to

"Thumpetty-thump-thump, look at Frosty go."

The pipes wheezed to a stop and the camel seemed to calm down. Then, as the men relaxed their grip, the animal raised his head to his full nine feet, lifted his nose into the air and spat directly at Mrs. Horst, who was leaning over her balcony rail viewing the festivities. It hit her directly in the face. Caught by surprise, Mrs. Horst yelped and threw herself backward against the opposite rail which, unfortunately, was not reinforced to the extent of holding someone of her particular girth. As the rail gave way and Mrs. Horst fell with a screech into a large haystack placed there to provide the animals with three days worth of fodder, another scream was heard from the crowd. It came from a mother holding her young son in her arms and covering his eyes. Before them was a sight that St. Germaine won't soon forget—a mature bull camel in full sexual arousal lit from beneath with the luminescent glow of a 40 watt manger.

"O my GOD!" said Meg amidst the gasps from the crowd. "O my GOD! How could...? Is that...? I just don't believe it!"

I was still trying to decide whether to shoot the bagpiper out of moral justification, but the sight of a male camel with love on its mind made me decide otherwise. If that camel got loose, anything I would do to the bagpiper, including shooting him, would be counted a blessing.

By this time, the entire cast of The Kiwanis Christmas had crossed the street to watch Seymour and his cohorts, all dressed as shepherds, trying to pull the camel from the staging area. Seymour has since told me that there is nothing quite so stubborn as a camel in full bloom, and it looked as though the twelve-hundred-pound animal wasn't going anywhere until its dreams of dromedary desire were fulfilled. Just then, Bertram, the St. Bernard puppy who had squeezed under the rail to see what all the commotion was, attached its jaws to the camel's hind leg, causing the animal to disregard all of its romantic notions and leave the stable at a dead run dragging a bevy of shepherds and the dog behind it down the snow covered street.

There wasn't much talking in the aftermath, most of the spectators being stunned to silence.

Suddenly, from the crowd, came a sweet little voice.

"Mommy, is that an angel?"

All eyes raised to the star on the pole above the manger, shining through the swirling snow and illuminating the feminine form hanging unsupported about six feet above the stable. It settled slowly. It was a naked woman with, as it said in the brochure, "many anatomical enchantments." Mrs. Horst, who had struggled uninjured to her feet, looked up, gave a thin wail and fainted.

"That one's mine, too," shouted Arlen from the back of the crowd.

Since it was now two degrees above zero with the wind begin-ning to pick up, *The Crèches of St. Germaine* was canceled due to the weather at 7:23 p.m. And because there was no break in the Arctic front expected and the forecast was for three feet of snow, the next two nights were canceled as well.

"I glad we didn't miss that one," said Meg on the way back to the cabin. "And to think you wanted to stay home and decorate the tree."

"We can still finish it I think. And I've been giving Archimedes about seven mice a day. He's due for a few."

"Where are you getting all the mice?"

"From Kent Muphee down in Boone. He can get frozen mice by the case. And don't ask. I don't know why he'd need them. Just that he can get them from his medical supplier. No formalde-hyde. Just frozen."

"So you have...?"

"Three cases in the freezer. About six hundred mice. Oh, and a bag of baby squirrels."

Chapter 19

My first shot missed, but my second hit Isabel in her right shoulder and spun her to the ground, causing her shot to go wild, hitting Denver Tweed in the leg and dropping her like a three-legged donkey on St. Swithen's Day. Two down with one lucky shot. Lucky for Isabel, that is. I was aiming for her head.

"You realize, of course, that this mystery series may actually be the worst thing ever written. And I'm not kidding."

Meg was scrolling through the chapters as I was putting the finishing touches on the tree.

I chomped thoughtfully on my R&J cigar, leaning out precariously on the ladder to place the star atop the now decorated conifer.

"I mean, *really*. A three-legged donkey on St. Swithen's Day?"

"Hmmm," I said, coming down the ladder and surveying the tree. "The choir seems to like it."

The tree looked pretty good.

"They just *said* they liked it to be kind. Besides, you have enough chapters to fill their choir folders from now till Pentecost. I suggest you wrap it up and start a new mystery in the spring."

"You just want me all to yourself," I said.

"You're such a clever lad," Meg said.

Archimedes had graduated from the kitchen to the living room. Although the frigid air didn't seem to bother him, he seemed to prefer the warmth of the fire and the plate of mousy snacks that Meg had left for him on the table. I had called my contractor and despite the cold weather and the Christmas season, gotten him to come out to the house and install an automatic window for lack of a better term—something of my own design. Archimedes could step up to the kitchen window, trigger the electric eye and the window would slide open, allowing

Archimedes access to the warmth of the house. Likewise, he could return to the wild at his leisure. It took no time at all for the owl to learn the trick and it saved leaving the window open for him to arrive. I must say, the first time I saw the bird gliding noiselessly through the house, finally landing on the head of the stuffed elk above the fireplace, I was speechless—as was Meg.

I looked quickly over to Amber Dawn, Personal Trainer. She had reached the gun but still looked as unsure about her options as a nun on a double date--options that were changing as quickly as the towel boy in the Vatican basketball locker room.

"Drop it, Amber. I don't want to shoot you."

"You wouldn't shoot me, would you handsome?" Amber squeaked, her lashes going into overdrive.

"In a heartbeat, sweetheart."

She didn't believe me, but I was telling the truth. I proved it a moment later.

"You killed Amber? Amber Dawn, Personal Trainer?"

I nodded. "She had to go. It was her or me."

"At least you spared us the gruesome details."

"She's dead all right. As dead as Morning Prayer."

Isabel groaned, got to her knees and tried to level her own gun at me without success. Denver wasn't moving.

"Don't do it Isabel. Or should I say 'Isadore.'"

"How...how did you know?" He dropped the gun, his shoulders slumping faster than Pete Rose at a poker party.

"I've known for years. I just chose to keep your secret. Isadore Gerhardt, famous cross-dressing music evangelist from Pascagoula, Mississippi. I caught your act at the Southern Baptist Convention in '74. I knew you were in love with Amber, but the only way she'd be with you was if you were the Bishop."

Suddenly, out of the corner of my eye, I saw a gigantic shape loom toward me. I spun on my heel and shot quickly, two shots without aiming, my .38 held tight against my hip. The two bullets hit Denver hard but barely slowed her down. She had pulled the leg loose from the piano and was getting ready to finish me when my next shot hit the mark. A puzzled look crossed her face as she sank to the floor.

"That's six," said Isadore with an evil grin as I stood contemplating the carnage. He picked his own gun back up off the floor, this time in his left hand.

"Six what?"

"Six bullets. Two at me. One at Amber. Three at Denver. Looks like your luck has run out, shoofly."

My gun was still in my hand as I mentally added the shots that I'd fired. He was right and he knew it. He raised his gun slowly so that I'd have time to reflect on my mistake for a final few seconds.

That's when I shot him. Unfortunately for Isadore, a Taurus .38 Special has seven chambers.

Rhiza showed up at exactly nine o'clock. I had the coffee made and was working on some of my famous omelets when she walked in. She was back in her society mode, trading the jeans and old sweatshirt of her last visit for the casual chic of J. Crew. Her hair was perfect as usual, her makeup, sublime. She looked like a million bucks.

"Have a seat," I said. "Breakfast is almost ready."

"I've missed these omelets. Are you sure you can't tell me your secret?"

"So you can give it to your cook? I think not."

Rhiza got up and poured herself a cup of coffee. "Warm you up?" she asked.

"I will presume you're referring to my coffee and answer in the affirmative." She giggled and filled my mug to the top, then returned to the table.

"I guess we should talk."

"I guess we should," I said putting her plate in front of her.

"You see, here's the thing…"

"Don't let your eggs get cold."

"OK. Hey," she said, suddenly remembering. "How's the owl?"

"He's great. I fixed the window so he can go in and out. He's out now, but he'll be back soon. He's discovered central heating."

She nodded and pushed her eggs around on the plate, not doing any serious damage.

"You see, here's the thing," she began again. I had a feeling this speech was rehearsed. I decided to be proactive as they say at the police academy.

"Listen, Rhiza. Are you having an affair with Loraine Ryan?"

"Um…no."

"No?"

She sighed. "The short answer is 'no.' The long answer is still 'no,' but a bit more complicated."

I waited for her to go on as I dug in, not wanting my own breakfast to get cold.

"Malcolm and I are having problems. You remember?"

"Mmhmm," I nodded in the affirmative, my mouth being full.

"Well, I started going in to Loraine for counseling. It was Malcolm's idea. He'd gone a few times and said she was wonderful. So I went."

I had finished my mouthful and took a sip of coffee. "And then what?"

"Then I found out he was sleeping with her."

"So you were telling the truth?"

"Yes, it was the truth. Sort of. You see, sleeping with her…it's part of her therapy."

"What?!"

"You know she's a trained therapist."

"I don't care if she's a trained seal! She *cannot* do that. You know better." I had stopped eating and was now just looking at

Rhiza in disbelief.

"I know it. But when you're in the sessions with her, she just makes it seem so...so...plausible, I guess. Like it's the right thing to do."

"And was this part of *your* therapy, too?"

"It was supposed to be. I was with her in her office around ten at night. Her door was locked, but then Willie came in using his pass key."

"Ah...then Willie came in."

"We hadn't done anything, but I admit it probably looked bad. I grabbed my stuff and got out of there fast. I haven't been back. Not for therapy anyway."

"Why would Malcolm tell me that you're having an affair with Loraine?"

"Probably because he's still going to sessions with her. I think he wanted to stop. I even begged him. But he's still seeing her twice a week. Now with this murder thing coming up again, I think that he knows you'll find out that Willie walked in on us. He wants you to know about it in advance and agree to keep it confidential. That way, he can keep seeing Loraine and I'm the bad girl. Unfortunately for Malcolm, he doesn't know our history." She paused. "Your eggs are getting cold," she added.

"How would I find out what Willie saw? I mean, I'm a good detective, but we've come up blank on just about everything."

"Because he told someone."

"Who? Who did he tell?"

"Willie was in love with Loraine. He sent her notes, followed her around like a puppy. When he walked in on Loraine and me, he got really angry."

"So who did he tell?"

"He told the bishop."

"He did what?!"

"He called the bishop and told him that Loraine and I were having an affair."

"That's grounds for Loraine's immediate dismissal. Why would he do that if he was in love with her?"

"He was mad at her. I guess he felt betrayed. Anyway, the bishop called Loraine and she denied the whole thing. So did I. Of course, I was only asked if I was having an affair with Loraine, which I wasn't. So it was Willie's word against hers. She filed a sexual harassment lawsuit as a smokescreen so it would make Willie's testimony less credible. But when the inquiry began and I was called to testify, I would have had to tell the truth. I told Malcolm as much."

"Why didn't the bishop come forward with this information?"

"Why would he? The complaint was acted on, the charges of an affair were denied by Loraine and myself, and then the complaining party up and got himself killed before the inquiry."

"This is just incredible."

"I guess the note on the organ was to throw another monkey-wrench into the works. I sure never thought that it would point to me though."

"Well, the convolution worked up to a point. Once we found out the cross was poisoned and figured out the anagram, it made us think that Loraine Ryan was the target when it was Willie all along. The bad thing for the killer is that it kept the case alive for two months when it probably would have disappeared by now. Another case of the incredibly clever criminal being too smart for his or her own britches."

Rhiza smiled for the first time since she arrived. "So who did it?"

"I'm going to call the bishop, you know, and check your story out."

"Of course you are. I'd expect nothing less."

"Then it's obvious who did it. It was Malcolm."

I caught her totally surprise.

"Malcolm?! No!"

"All right," I said, laughing. "I'm just kidding. It was Loraine.

She must have seen him playing with that cross on any number of occasions and probably told him to just take it, knowing it would finally end up in his mouth. But Malcolm sure knew about it. Still and all, proving it is going to be something else again."

It was a stretch and I knew it.

The Sunday morning before Christmas was usually a big service for the choir and this year was no exception. The Liturgy of the Word, or the first half of the service, was to be the traditional English Lessons and Carols. However, due to the length of the service and the Eucharist that was to follow, the traditional nine lessons had been trimmed to six. The choir had four anthems to sing, along with carol arrangements and service music. Herself, if she was hearing any footsteps behind her, didn't look nervous or preoccupied in the least. It was a fine service, if I do say so myself. The anthems would have to do double duty on Christmas Eve because rehearsal time was at a premium this time of year. On Christmas Eve, our musical program began at 10:30 followed by the Christmas Mass at 11:00.

On Monday I went shopping. I usually waited till Christmas Eve to do my shopping, but this year, it looked like Christmas Eve was going to be busier than usual.

I went into Boone to pick up the presents I'd found for the McCollough kids. For Bud, a bottle of Deloach Reserve Estate and a Ravenswood Mendocino, two Zinfandels that would age nicely in the next five or six years. Then a good looking first baseman's mitt, a couple of baseballs and the *Lord of the Rings* trilogy, which he said he hadn't read yet. For Pauli Girl, some doll stuff and some clothes that Meg picked out and had on hold at several different stores. A lot of clothes. And for Moosey, a BMX bike, the Harry Potter books, and a new jacket. I didn't get Ardine anything. The one time I did, a few years ago, she didn't know how to act around me for months. So now I just take care of the kids. It's probably all she wants for Christmas anyway.

I stopped at a little farm on my way up to Boone to check on Megan's present, a present that I wouldn't retrieve until Christmas Eve. I also checked in with Dave at the station. Nothing going on. I spent the rest of the day and most of the evening on the Willie Boyd case.

On Tuesday morning I decided I had puzzled enough. I couldn't come up with any way to prove that Loraine had killed Willie Boyd. I had gone through a lot of plans that included, but were not limited to:

• Confiscating her computer and looking for undeleted notes that would implicate her—a virtual impossibility. Even if she was stupid enough to leave them on her computer, which I doubted, her office was always open and anyone could have gone in and written them.

• Trying to trick her into confessing—"Yes, I admit it. You tricked me. I'm the one who killed him! If only you weren't as incredibly smart as you are handsome, I would have gotten away with it." The chances of this happening were slim and none and slim was out of town.

• Somehow luring her into somehow doing or saying something only the murderer would know, thus hoisting her on her own petard. Although this works on *Matlock*, it's generally not enough to convict anyone and I had nothing but bad circumstantial evidence. Dead hedgehogs, a reference to a love note that Willie may or may not have written and a clue that didn't actually point to the murderer.

I had to go with plan B.

Chapter 20

I put a call though to the Bishop from my cell phone—first routing it through the St. Germaine police department to give it the appropriate caller ID—while sitting in my truck directly outside the Bishop's diocesan office at about 11:00 on Tuesday, December twenty-third. I got his secretary. Bishop Douglas' office was a good three hour drive from St. Germaine, but I had found out he was still in town and had left early, enjoying a leisurely breakfast on the road.

"I'm sorry Mr. Konig. Bishop Douglas is out of the office until January the twenty-second."

"That's quite a little vacation."

She sniffed. "The Bishop works very hard as I'm sure you know."

"I'm sure he does. Do you have his home number?"

"He prefers not to be disturbed."

"This is *Detective* Konig of the St. Germaine police department. I'm calling in regard to a homicide investigation and I would like a return phone call from Bishop Douglas within the next five minutes or I'm coming down there with a warrant, confiscate his computer, and take his office apart. Now, do you need my number?"

"No, it's on the caller ID."

"Thank you. I'll expect his call shortly."

I opened the coffee that I'd picked up at Starbucks and waited for the return call while I listened to the Mendelssohn *Christus*. It was his unfinished oratorio, but the Christmas choruses were wonderful. I was about halfway through *There Shall A Star From Jacob Come Forth* when the phone call rang and I answered.

"Hayden. It's Dave. He's on the line."

"Go ahead and put him through."

I listened and heard "He's right here. Just a moment." Then I came on.

"Hello, George. I'd like to meet with you. Today."

"I'm sorry, Hayden, I'm not available today. Perhaps you could make an appointment with Frances."

"Are you at your house?"

"Why, yes I am, but..."

"Perhaps I didn't make myself clear, George. I have come into some information about Willie Boyd's murder. This information concerns you and I think you'd better meet with me or my next call is to the Presiding Bishop's Office, followed by the office of the Council of Bishops. And I can pretty much guarantee that the newspapers won't be far down the line."

"Why don't we meet, Hayden? I can see you at about four."

"That'll be fine. I can't even leave St. Germaine for another hour," I said, hanging up.

It wasn't a long wait. The Bishop showed up in about fifteen minutes. I gave him about three minutes—just enough time to fire up his computer—then I followed him into the office.

"Hi, Frances, the Bishop in?" I asked as I pushed past her, opened the door and found him hunched over his keyboard typing in his password.

"It seems my timing is impeccable," I said, putting my coffee down on his desk and pulling his chair back away from the keyboard. "A warrant will be here shortly but we don't need you to take anything off the computer that might pertain to this investigation." I was lying about the warrant.

"You can't—you won't—" he sputtered, standing in indignation.

"Just sit down, George. It's time for us to have a talk. Or rather for me to talk. You can just listen, if you like."

"I know that Loraine Ryan killed Willie Boyd. I also know that you not only knew that, but did not come forth with this information."

"Priest and penitent privilege," he ventured, still rattled.

"Are you saying that Loraine confessed to this murder to you? It hardly seems like something she'd do."

"I'm prepared to say that she did."

"You're prepared to say that she confessed to the murder?"

"No...What I mean is...that, well, if she *did* confess to the murder, which I'm not saying she did, then I couldn't tell you about it. So I'm not. Telling you, that is."

Matlock's got nothing on yours truly. But it wasn't information I could use and I knew it. I gave him a minute to get his thoughts back on track.

"She didn't confess, did she?"

He sighed. "No. No, she didn't."

"But you knew."

"Not for sure. I didn't know for sure. She's my first female appointment and I needed her to be good. Not just good—great. I thought she was golden. She was great in seminary, but she's been nothing but trouble. That ReImagining Conference was awful. I've never heard of such things."

"You *did* know about the sex."

"Willie Boyd called me. But I couldn't take the word of a drunken janitor over a priest, a senior warden and his wife."

"You never asked the right questions. And you sure didn't follow up on it." I was beginning to feel sorry for him. "When Willie was killed, you should have looked a lot harder. You knew she had something to do with it."

He closed his eyes and nodded, his right hand holding tightly to the cross around his neck. I sat back and took a sip of the coffee.

"Look here, George," I continued, not unkindly. "You know as well as I do that she *cannot* stay at St. Barnabas, but more than that, you can't even let her remain a priest."

He opened his eyes and looked out the window at nothing in particular, his eyes unfocused.

"Rhiza Walker is ready and willing to testify concerning

Loraine Ryan's 'sexual healing' practices with herself and her husband in Loraine's private counseling sessions. That is out of bounds in every conceivable way and she should be defrocked. I'm not going to arrest her for murder—quite frankly I don't have enough evidence—but she has to go. Today. You have all the evidence that you need for a hearing if she insists on one, but I suspect she won't. Make no mistake—if she remains in the priesthood, I will go to the council of Bishops and lay this out before them, including your part in all this."

"What about Willie Boyd? This is something I'll carry with me to my grave."

"Pray for forgiveness, George. If it's any consolation to you, Willie had less than six months to live anyway. He had a bad heart."

"It's no consolation. That man's life is on my head." He looked ten years older.

"You announced that you were planning to stay another year before you retired. I suggest that you take your pension and retire now...for health reasons."

He nodded.

"I expect that Loraine Ryan will be gone by the time I get back to St. Germaine."

"I expect she will."

"Merry Christmas, George."

He didn't answer. His eyes closed again and his hand was clutching the cross around his neck. His lips were moving silently.

"You can erase your computer disk now if you want."

I got to the courthouse in Asheville at about 2:00 in the afternoon. It took almost an hour to find what I was searching for. With the document firmly in hand, I headed for home. It was a day well spent.

Christmas Eve

Chapter 21

I had called Tony Brown, our retired priest, on the way back from my meeting with the bishop and filled him in on the goings on. He agreed to be the celebrant for the Christmas Eve service since he was planning on being there anyway. Past that, he had no plans to return, even on a part-time basis, but indicated that he might fill in on occasion until we found a new priest.

I never saw Loraine Ryan leave. Nor did anyone else I talked to. I didn't get up to the church to practice until Wednesday night and by then her office was cleaned out and she was gone. Marilyn was off for the afternoon and didn't know Loraine was gone until Thursday morning. Christmas Eve was always a half-day for the staff and was generally taken up with opening various gifts which were brought in by the parishioners and other staff members.

I filled Dave, Nancy, and Meg in on the case when I returned to town, but cautioned them not to say anything. We'd just let it go, but leave the case file open—the unsolved murder at St. Barnabas. Rhiza informed me later that day that she and Malcolm had decided to separate, but were going to try to work things out. She was going to try one of the Baptist churches in Boone for a while—mainly because she found out that they had installed some tanning beds in their family life center.

"Dark am I, yet lovely, O daughters of Jerusalem, dark like the tents of Kedar, like the tent curtains of Solomon," Rhiza quoted. "Do not stare at me because I am dark, because I am dark-ened by the sun."

It seemed to me that she had done her research just a little too well. However, I had to admit that a Biblical Literalist might agree that her quotation from the *Song of Solomon* could be loosely construed as an admonition directly from the Old Testament that we should all strive to have nice tans. In defense of orthodoxy, I also mentioned to her that the Southern Baptists hardly ever read the *Song of Solomon* except on marriage encounter weekend retreats—and only then behind closed doors with the lights out.

Your stature is like that of the palm, and your breasts like clusters of fruit.

I said, "I will climb the palm tree; I will take hold of its fruit."

"Brother Dan says that we shouldn't have to go out to a secular tanning facility just to obey the scriptures," Rhiza said. "It's obvious that God has a plan for my life. No visible tan lines."

I pondered Rhiza's No-Tan-Line Theological Construct as I drove past the manger scenes still decorating Main Street on my way to the church on Thursday morning. The snow drifts were about three feet high inside the stables and some smart-alec, who shall remain nameless, had placed a dozen two-foot high plastic penguins around the Kiwanis Club manger. It wasn't my fault. Archie McPhee and Co., outfitters of popular culture, had them on sale.

The family service at 5:30 was packed—as it always was. The choir didn't sing but Father Brown did a nice children's sermon, the retelling of the Christmas Story and a lot of congregational singing. I noticed that Ardine and her kids were in the front row sitting next to Nancy. At the 11:00 service, the choir would sing the Charpentier *Midnight Mass* as well as several anthems during communion including the "Moldy Cheese" madrigal, and would end with the traditional *Silent Night* after which Meg and I would head over to the McCollough's with the presents for the kids.

The Eucharist finished up around seven and I had told Megan I'd meet her at the cabin after the service. She was there waiting for me, looking beautiful in a red velvet dress.

"Like it? It's my Christmas Eve dress."

"Stunning," I said, meaning it.

"Here's your present," she said, handing me a nicely wrapped box. "You know, you're incredibly difficult to buy for."

"I know what this is," I said, opening the package and expecting the leather bomber jacket that I had hinted about for weeks. It was empty.

"Hey, what's the deal?"

"I didn't want to get you just any old thing. Go look in your study."

I walked through the living room into the old two story cabin and there standing in the corner, a full six feet tall, was a stuffed buffalo.

"No WAY! This is GREAT! Where on earth did you get such a thing?"

"There was a restaurant going out of business in Chapel Hill. I do the investments for the owner. So I made him a offer he couldn't refuse."

"How did you get it in here?"

"A few choir members lent their muscle to the task."

"Well, I must say that this is the finest present I've ever received," I said taking her in my arms and kissing her soundly.

"Hmmm. Aren't you forgetting something?" Meg was nothing, if not direct.

"Ah yes. Wait here for a second. I'll be right back. You can give Archimedes a few mice while you wait." The owl had been sitting patiently on the table since I'd come in, but now was looking around the room in consternation for his dinner.

I disappeared out the back door and reappeared a few moments later with a wriggling bundle that I could barely hold on to. Finally I put him down and he was in Meg's arms before I could say "Merry Christmas."

"I LOVE him!" Meg said, sitting on the floor, the six-week old puppy dancing all over her new dress.

"He's a Burmese Mountain Dog. Very loyal, and a good watchdog."

Archimedes had retreated to the elk head to eat his mouse, but otherwise didn't seem too ruffled at the prospect of another animal in the house.

"By the way, you see that little cask around his neck?"

"Yes, it's SO cute!"

"Well, my dear, open it up."

Meg opened the end of the cask and pulled out a strand of Australian pearls.

"Wow. They're beautiful. I don't know what to say. Thank you." She eyed me suspiciously. "Are they real?"

"Of course they're real. I am a millionaire, you know."

"I love them!" she said, putting on the pearls and turning her attention back to the puppy. "What should I name the little rascal?"

"How about Mr. Peepers?"

"Oh shut up. I'll have to think about it. He needs just the right name."

"Well, think about it," I said. "You'll come up with something. Merry Christmas."

"Merry Christmas to you."

And it was.

Chapter 22

I waited till Ardine's kids were back in school and the Beautiful Snow Princess of December had morphed itself into the Howling Ice-Beast of January before I decided to go back over to her trailer. It was snowing heavily as I drove up, parked my truck and knocked on her front door.

"Hi, Ardine," I said as she opened the door, at the same time stomping the snow off of my boots. "May I come in?"

"I suppose."

"I have a couple of things to show you."

I walked into the living room and put the paper grocery bag I was carrying onto the kitchen table, then shook my arms free of my coat and dropped it over the back of the chair.

"May I sit down?" I said, sitting down.

Ardine shrugged, sat across from me and watched me nervously, her hands folded in front of her, resting on the table.

"I have some things here you might be interested in."

I opened the bag and began to put some items on the table. A half-smoked cigar, two bottles of wine, a matchbook, an old skeleton key and a thirty year old census report.

"It seems," I started, watching her eyes dart back and forth from object to object. "It seems that Willie Boyd had a half-brother. I had to go to the census figures from 1970 to find him. Did you know that Willie was your husband PeeDee's half-brother? Course you did. PeeDee's father was Roger McCollough and Willie's father was Percy Boyd. Both born in Watauga County. Their mother, Emma, was married to Roger for only a year or two. Percy came along later a couple of years later, but she never married him."

"Look here," I said, pushing the census report across the table to Ardine, who made no move to take it. "Census report from 1970. Emma McCollough, single mother. Her two boys were living with her. Peter Dennis McCollough, age thirteen—That'd be PeeDee— and William Raymond Jefferson Boyd, age eleven.

Ardine was chewing on her bottom lip. She didn't say anything.

"I'm sure that Willie probably told you if you didn't know before."

I pushed the half-smoked cigar to the center of the table.

"This is the cigar that Willie left up in the choir loft where he died. I took it down to the coroner and guess what? The end was probably soaked in boiled oleander leaves just like the cross. I suspect that it wasn't the cross gave him the heart attack at all. It would have taken him quite a while to get a fatal dose unless he just sucked on it like a candy cane, and although he was a strange fellow, I doubt that he'd go quite that far. Anyway, he died pretty quickly."

Ardine sat quietly.

"Oh, I don't doubt that the Loraine Ryan wanted him dead and she surely dipped that cross in the mixture that JJ was cooking up, but I don't think that the cross killed Willie Boyd."

With one finger I slid the green book of matches with 'Pine Valley Christmas Tree Farm' emblazoned across the front across the table.

"These were beside the cigar up in the choir loft. That's where you work, isn't it, Ardine?"

"A lot of people come by there."

"Yes, they do. But the Pine Valley Tree Farm hasn't had these match books for a couple of years. Wonder where he found this one? I'll bet that if I looked around the trailer, I'd come up with another book or two."

"Don't know."

I pushed the two bottles of wine to the center of the table.

"These were in Willie's room. The interesting thing is, is that no dealer in the state of North Carolina even sells this kind of wine. They're Portuguese red wines. Not very expensive, but a good value for someone who collects. You can get it on the internet if you know where to look and if you have a credit card. Now why would Willie buy wine on the internet?"

"I don't know."

"I suspect that Willie didn't even know how to turn on a computer, much less know how to find a rare Portuguese wine and order it. Not to mention the fact that he didn't even have a bank account or a credit card. Doesn't Bud have a bank account?"

"I suppose."

"And a debit card?"

"I don't know."

I held up the old, brown skeleton key.

"This is the key that I found in Bud's room. Remember? It's the key to the wine closet at St. Barnabas. It came off of Willie's key ring. He was here a lot, wasn't he?"

I looked at Ardine for a full minute without saying anything. Her head was down and her hands remained locked on the table in a prayerful position as if she was getting ready to say grace.

"Look, Ardine. I already know what happened. Just tell me why."

"Do I need a lawyer?"

I studied her for a moment before making up my mind.

"No."

She nodded and said "I'm believin' you on that." Then she took a deep breath.

"Willie came by here about six months ago. He tole me that he knew that I killed PeeDee and he knew how I did it and that he was gonna tell the police. Then the police would come and put my kids in a home. I grew up in a home. I'm not lettin' them put my kids in one," she said angrily.

"Did you kill PeeDee?"

She pointed her finger at me and looked right into my eyes with new fire in her voice.

"I ain't sayin'. But things are different here in the hollers than they are down in town. You know that."

Her voice got quieter.

"Anyway, Willie started comin' by here every couple of mornin's after the kids got on the bus. I guess he didn't dare do it before Moosey started goin' to school. Anyway, he'd make me...you know...him and me.... And then he'd take off for work leavin' me sick to my stomach and feeling like dirt. I'd go take a shower but I felt like I couldn't even scrub his filthy stink off me."

She picked up one of the bottles.

"He stole those bottles from Bud, I guess. I seen 'em in his room. The judge said Bud wasn't s'pposed to have any wine and those bottles were under his bed. But he used his own newspaper money, so I didn't say anything to him. Willie was stealing other stuff from us, too. He took one of my quilts down to Boone and sold it for twenty dollars," she said in disgust. "Twenty dollars. And then was laughin' about it."

"And?"

"Willie tole me he was dyin' but I didn't believe him."

"He was telling the truth. He had maybe three or four months left."

"I just couldn't stand it anymore," she said, her hands shaking. "When JJ came around asking about the oleander, I had the idea. He left his cigars here one morning..."

"That's enough," I said, interrupting her. "Don't tell me any more. It wouldn't do for me me to hear it."

"I ain't sorry."

"Listen Ardine," I said.

"Yeah?"

"As far as the law is concerned, Willie died from the poison on that cross."

She looked across the table at me as I put the cigar and the matches back into the bag. I dropped the key into my pocket and left the wine and the census report on the table.

"So don't go killing anyone else."

Ardine nodded.

"Especially me," I added as an afterthought.

"I won't."

Postlude

Chapter 23

"Marilyn," I snarled over the phone. "I've got three dead people up here and I still have to pick the hymns for next week."

"So what else is new?" she answered. "I'll send up the janitors."

I sat down at my desk, pulled my hat low over my eyes and lit up a stogie. This was one for the books, all right, and I knew the Bishop well enough to know that he'd clean up the mess. I buzzed Marilyn back.

"Hey darlin', how 'bout some Java? This cigar tastes like a plumber's handkerchief."

"Come down and get it yourself," she purred.

"I'm on my way."

"And, by the way, there's someone here to see you. She says she's an alto."

"What's she wearing?"

"Hmmm," hummed Marilyn. "Wouldn't you like to know?"

The End

Raymond Chandler would be proud.

About the Author

Mark Schweizer, in varying stages of his career, has waited tables, performed in opera and oratorio, earned a doctorate, taught in college music departments, raised hedgehogs, directed church choirs, sung the bass solo to Beethoven's 9th with Robert Shaw and the Atlanta Symphony, hosted a classical music radio show, started a music publishing company, taught in a seminary, sung recitals, attempted to cash in on the potbellied pig boom of the 80s, run a regional opera company, composed church anthems, taught voice lessons, built a log cabin, written opera librettos, directed stage productions, helped his wife to raise their two children and managed to remain married for twenty-four years. He also owns several chainsaws.

"Well," Donis says, "it's never boring..."